Jesse grasped c palm. "Tell Sol what exactly as he says." Then he let her hand slip from his, and his expression hardened. "And don't come back here."

She knew his harsh words were his way of protecting her. But not seeing him or knowing he was all right would be a far worse fate than anything else she could imagine.

Footsteps echoed at her back.

"Whoever heard of a female reporter anyway?" Jesse mocked loudly. "You women should stay at home where you belong and leave the running of the world to us men."

"Like you men are doing such a great job. Besides, you're big news, cowboy. And we women have only begun to take our place in the thick of things. You might as well get accustomed to having me around."

Jesse balled his hands into fists, and he wore an expression of frustration—her message had gotten through loud and clear. On impulse she mouthed the words, *I love you*.

"Sheriff, get this female out of here. And in the future, I demand you keep her away from me." His voice was cold, but she hoped the fire in his eyes spoke of remembered passion, and not anger.

Sheriff Langford grabbed her elbow and escorted her non-too-gently away from the cell.

Praise for Gini Rifkin and...

TRAPPER'S MOON
~Winner, Reader's Choice Award, *Still Moments Magazine*
~5 Stars from N.N. Light Book Heaven

COWBOYS, CATTLE, AND CUTTHROATS
~Finalist, Colorado Romance Writers' Beverley Award
~4 Stars from NetGalley

A COWBOY'S FATE
~5 Stars from *Still Moments Magazine*
~Winner of Maple Leaf Award, best short story
~5 Stars from NetGalley

SPECIAL DELIVERY
~5 Stars and Publisher's Pick from *Still Moments Magazine*
~5 Stars from Fall Into Reading Reviews

SOLACE: Fae Warriors Book 1
~5 Stars from N.N. Light Book Heaven
~Finalist, Paranormal, Romance Guild Reviewer's Choice Award

BLISS: Fae Warriors Book 2
~5+ stars from N.N. Light Book Heaven

PORTENCE: Fae Warriors Book 3
"Great ending to a spectacular trilogy!"
~5 Stars from N. N. Light Book Heaven

Undercover Outlaw

by

Gini Rifkin

1-5-2021

For Mona
Best Wishes
gini Rifkin

Undercover Outlaw

Cover Art by *The Wild Rose Press, Inc.*

The Wild Rose Press, Inc.
PO Box 708
Adams Basin, NY 14410-0708
Visit us at www.thewildrosepress.com

Publishing History
First Cactus Rose Edition, 2020
Trade Paperback ISBN 978-1-5092-3404-2
Digital ISBN 978-1-5092-3405-9

Published in the United States of America

Dedication

For Gary, always. And family and friends.
Thank you once again to the Wild Rose Press,
the amazing Amanda Barnett,
and my technical advisor for everything horsey,
Carol Ledbetter.

Other books by this author...
The Dragon and The Rose
Lady Gallant
Iron Heart
Special Delivery
Victorian Dream
A Cowboy's Fate
Cowboys, Cattle, and Cutthroats
Trapper's Moon
~*~

Fae Warrior Series:
Solace
Bliss
Portence
~*~

Australia Burns, Volume Two
(Show Australia Some Love, Book 2)
Waiting for Caleb

Chapter One

Prairie Ridge, Colorado, late spring, 1888

"What in tarnation is wrong with you?"

With his hat pulled low and his face partially covered with a blue bandana, only the man's dark eyes were visible.

"Didn't Solomon instruct you on what to do during the hold up?"

Frozen with fear, Trinity stared back, too stunned to answer. Besides, the man's words made no sense. Who in the blazes was Solomon?

He poked at the brim of a dusty Stetson with the business end of his revolver. The hat slid back, revealing black eyebrows now flattened into a scowl.

"Put these in your hatbox and give me the money." He produced a fistful of papers from beneath his vest. "Then pretend to be scared like the rest of the women."

Pretend to be scared? She was terrified, but she wasn't about to relinquish her money or her chance at freedom to this two-bit bandit. She drew back her arm and landed a right cross to his jaw. Pain exploded in her knuckles and radiated up her arm. Hitting a side of beef couldn't have hurt more.

His eyes flickered, but he didn't flinch. "That's more than enough realism." He glanced back at the other outlaws. "Your overacting is going to get us both killed." Unsuccessfully, he tried to stuff the documents under the lid of the hatbox clutched to her chest.

Overacting? Why did this man behave as if she should know him? Maybe outlaws were just loco by nature.

Afraid for her life, she edged toward the shelter of the stagecoach. But as she turned to climb aboard, the outlaw grabbed and spun her around. Her beautiful hatbox flew from her grasp. A kaleidoscope of color, it tumbled along the ground, missing a puddle by an inch before slamming to a halt up against a clump of sagebrush. Carrying twenty years' worth of special memories, the box represented her entire life. Anger replaced every drop of fear.

"Let me go, you dimwit." She struggled against the man and slapped at his face, her fingers tangling in the blue cloth. The fabric loosened and fell down around his neck. With a growl of frustration, he secreted the papers back beneath his vest.

A second masked man hurried over—gun drawn. "Damn it to hell, Jesse. She done seen what you look like. Now you'll have to kill her."

At the gravity of the words, Trinity's heart seemed to stop, then it raced forward in double time. She shifted her gaze back to the man who had just been appointed her executioner.

He swore under his breath. "And thanks to you, now she knows my name."

In desperation, she glanced at the stagecoach driver and the other passengers. The men and other women, herded off to one side by the other outlaws, huddled beneath a tree, too far away to help or to even hear what was happening to her.

"Do it and be quick about it," the second man ordered. "We gotta get out of here." He cocked the hammer back on his forty-five and pointed the weapon at her head. Then he made the sound of a gun firing. When she jumped, he laughed like an addlebrained drunk.

The man named Jesse jerked her up against his chest. "Maybe I'll just keep her a while. I'm the only one up at the hideout without a woman." His gaze appeared troubled, but his mouth slanted into a leer as he leaned closer, angling his body between her and the other bandit.

"Whatever you're gonna do," the second outlaw warned, "do it now."

Trinity's mind went blank. She didn't know whether to scream, faint, or cuss a blue streak. Her disposition favored cussing, but her body had other ideas.

****

Jesse holstered his gun and studied the girl.

Aww no—there she went. Her face turned white as a salt flat, and her eyes rolled back as she crumpled toward the ground. He caught her with one arm and held her against his hip.

Now he was in a real mess, and so was she. Shifting his hands to her midriff, he hefted her up and over his shoulder. Thankfully, she was slight of build.

Sidestepping, he flexed at the knees and retrieved the satin and lace monstrosity of a hatbox. He'd waited weeks for the opportunity to pass this information on to Denver, and to pick up the marked money from Sol. If he got caught with either, things would go real bad for everybody involved.

Glaring past the skirt and petticoat fluttering and flapping across his chest and face, he strode over to where the other outlaws waited—already saddled up and anxious to ride.

"Fresh blood?" Another of the outlaws handed off the reins to Jesse's horse.

"She's mine, Dooley. You got your own piece of fluff." Jesse looped the pink satin ribbon of the hatbox over the saddle horn and quickly deposited the girl across the horse in front of the saddle. His mount grunted, none too happy with the off-kilter load. "And in the morning, this one takes a one-way trip to Blue Mesa Canyon, if you get my drift."

The other man grunted in understanding.

A web of guilt tightened around Jesse's conscience. He hadn't meant to hurt anyone, hadn't meant to put anyone in danger. All he wanted was justice—justice and revenge.

Clutching a handful of the girl's long blonde hair, he tilted her head and studied her face. The color had returned to her cheeks, but she was still out cold. He jerked the bandana from around his neck, and folding the fabric into a long tail, tied the cloth across her eyes. Hopefully it would keep her calm when she came to— the method worked with horses. And the less she knew about where she was going and who was involved, the better things would be for the both of them.

As he reached for the length of rope in his saddlebag, his guts tightened. Disgusted at the idea of tying her up, he jammed the twist of hemp back into the pack, hoping the other outlaws hadn't noticed the show of mercy.

"Let's ride." Billy Bart, their leader, prodded the

gang into action. Hooting in victory, and shooting their pistols into the air, they took off in a cloud of dust.

Jesse shoved the hatbox aside and swung up into the saddle. His roan gelding, eager to follow, leaped forward, churning rock and dust beneath his hooves.

The hatbox banged against his knee, and the female's calico-covered bottom bounced up and down in front of him. Cursing, he drew the young woman's limp form up over the saddle horn and tight against his stomach to cushion her from the jarring ride. His arm cradled softness, but her hip bone pressed noticeably up against the front of his trousers—the repeated contact inspiring unexpected results.

Jesse reined in his horse. "Go on ahead," he called to the nearest man. "I'll be along in a minute. I need to—rearrange the load."

He let the young woman's body sag down over the horse while he adjusted the fit of his Levi's. Then he lugged her upright to sit in front of him.

"Wake up." He jostled her and urged his horse into a walk.

She moaned and stiffened in his arms—then reached for the blindfold.

"Leave it on, or I'll tie you up as well."

Her hands stilled in midair. Then she groped at his chest, latching onto the front of his shirt. "Why are you doing this? Where are you taking me?"

"Hush up." If only he'd had the sense to gag her. "The why should be obvious, and you're better off not knowing where."

She clamped her mouth shut, but alarm and anger seemed to radiate from her body.

A breeze riffled through her unbound hair, sending

a strand of gold playing across his cheek. A sweet fragrance followed, calling up memories of simple pleasures and times gone by. He shifted, trying to get comfortable, and she trembled in his arms, small and delicate as a newborn foal. The rise and fall of her chest pressed against his. She was breathing too fast.

Angling his head back, he studied her profile.

Her nib of a nose barely peeked out from beneath the bandana, and her lips were full and puckered like those of a frightened child fighting not to cry. She didn't look like any hooker he'd ever met. She must be an actress—although, so far, her performance left quite a bit to be desired. He supposed Sol hadn't found much to choose from in the backwaters of Colorado.

Gingerly, he touched the fingertips of one hand to his bruised jaw, opening and closing his mouth a few times, making sure everything still worked. Regardless of her occupation, she'd delivered a surprisingly good punch.

"You sure got us in a fine mess," he muttered.

"Me?" She tightened her grip on his shirt. "This is all your fault. And I demand you release me— immediately."

She struggled in his arms. Her elbow caught him in the gut, and her head just missed slamming into his chin. "It's too late for that. Thanks to you, we've no choice but to play this out to the end."

"But I didn't do anything. Please. You can trust me. I won't tell anyone who you are or what you look like."

What the heck was the matter with this woman? Something just wasn't right here.

"Listen to me." He tightened his grip to still her

movements and emphasize his words. "Those men up ahead will be watching the two of us, and if I just let you go, they'll make it their business to track you down and kill you. So tonight, you're going to do exactly what I say—when I say. No questions asked. Do you understand?"

She swallowed hard and nodded.

"I hope that you do, because your life depends on it."

And so might his. He was already ass deep in sidewinders, not the snakes, but the human kind, and now this. One false move and they could both end up dead.

"What did Solomon tell you to do once you reached Denver?" He needed to know how much she knew about the whole setup.

She hesitated and licked her lips. "I can't remember."

How could she not remember? On the other hand, why would she lie to him? He exhaled around a snarl of frustration. She cringed at the sound, like a pup who had known a rough hand in the raising. The reflex action appeared ingrained and long-standing, and sympathy for her plight gained a shaky foothold—but he fought the emotion. Sentimentality wasn't something he could afford to indulge in right now.

His horse perked up its ears and stepped lively as they veered off the main road and onto the trail leading to the hideout. The abandoned farm up ahead had once belonged to a wealthy Easterner, now gone even farther west. Well-appointed, the dwelling offered comfortable living for the ill-mannered boys who worked for Mr. Briggs.

At the gate to the property, Jesse slowed their pace. They passed beneath the high wooden arch. The name Angels' Retreat could barely be read in the weathered sign attached to the lofty timber. Devil's Boardinghouse seemed a more fitting name.

The other men were already inside, leaving their mounts standing neglected in the corral. They ran them hot and then left them sweaty and saddled up and shivering in the breeze. Without a care for anyone or anything, they were as wild as this wide-open country—no boundaries and no one but the boss to tell them no.

Dismounting near the barn, Jesse reached up, grasped the girl around the waist, and lowered her to the ground. Her body glided down the front of his. She might not weigh much, but she was all woman. These days, such softness seemed foreign to him.

As her feet touched the ground, she gasped and stumbled backward. He clamped one hand around her upper arm, holding her in place. With the other he unhooked the hatbox from the saddle horn and set the box on the ground. Old Thomas, the grizzled ranch-worker who cared for the horses and lived in the barn, ambled out the door.

Jesse turned toward the older man. "Howdy, Thomas. Be sure Webster gets fresh water and a good rubdown, will you?" He handed the man a twenty-five-cent piece.

"Yes, sir. Thank you, Jesse. I won't forget." The man led the gelding inside, eyeing the woman but not saying anything. Jesse figured the money would go toward drink, but Thomas took good care of the animals, and who was he to judge the man.

"What's your name?" Jesse asked, tired of thinking of her as the woman.

"Trinity," she said, her voice no louder than a mouse squeak.

"What?"

"Oh, for heaven's sake," she muttered irritably. "Trinity. T-r-i-n-i-t-y."

That was the strangest name he'd ever heard for a female. But he thought better of saying so. She seemed ill-tempered enough as it was.

His gaze lingered on her parted lips, then drifted downward. At least she was easy on the eyes. Maybe being forced to spend the night with her wouldn't be so bad after all. Who was he kidding? Of course, it was going to be bad. Just spending a short amount of time with her had put him through enough aggravation and worry to last a lifetime.

She canted her head back trying to peek out from beneath the blindfold. He shoved the rumpled cloth farther down over her face. Her lips tightened into an angry line. Then she opened her mouth, no doubt ready to cut loose with her temper.

"The less you know the better, remember? So quit asking for trouble."

To his relief, she held her silence.

He secured the ribbon of the hatbox over her free arm, and then marched her to the big house. After navigating the foyer, he dragged her down the hallway to the parlor.

The dust-laden outlaws lounged on the tattered velvet-covered furniture. Feet up, their spurs dug deep troughs into the low teakwood table-tops, and their cigar ashes left mottled gray patches on the worn

Persian rug. Jesse grabbed a plate of food off the sideboard. "See you in the morning, boys." Turning, he headed toward the stairs to his room.

Cat calls and wolf whistles followed him. Even the cook/houseboy grinned knowingly.

"If she's too much woman for ya," one man taunted, "just give me a holler."

"If anybody's going to need help," Jesse called over his shoulder, "it'll be her."

Trinity stopped dead in her tracks and strained against his grip. He felt as if someone had handed him a bag of dynamite—short-fused, lit, and ready to blow.

"Settle down," he ordered, out of the side of his mouth. "And pick up your feet. There's a flight of stairs in front of you."

Not giving her a choice, he propelled her forward up the steps and into his room. He nudged the door shut with his foot, set the plate of food on the dresser, and after relieving her of the hatbox pushed her up against the bed.

"Sit," he said gruffly, "and leave the blindfold on."

For some reason, he didn't want to see her eyes, although he recalled they were blue. At least their exact shade eluded him. He didn't need to know if they were warm like forget-me-nots, or a freezing blue/gray like a high mountain lake. And he didn't want to know if there was fear in them. It would only make his job all the harder, and the task before him was already damn near impossible.

He lit the wick on the kerosene lamp.

She was no bigger than a minute, but she guaranteed him trouble for at least the next twenty-four hours. Just look at her. She was scared to death—yet there was open defiance in her posture and pure stubbornness in the set of her mouth—a mouth, more tempting than any he'd bothered to notice in quite some time. Unfortunately, defiance and stubbornness could be a dangerous combination.

Didn't she realize the jeopardy she had put them in? Question after question harried through his mind, but he didn't dare demand answers from her now. Not when he thought he heard footfalls outside his door.

He reached for the food. "Here." He placed the plate in her lap and fork in her hand. Her fingers were like ice, and his anger cooled a few degrees. "Eat up. It's a long time 'til morning."

He hung his hat on a wall peg and grabbed a piece of jerky and hardtack from the spare saddle pack he'd left hanging across the back of a chair earlier that day. Chewing on the leathery meat, he watched her fumble with the fork and then resort to using her fingers. She sampled the first bite tentatively then tore into the remainder of the food as if this was the first decent meal she'd had in a while.

She must be one of those starving actresses.

And what was her name...Trinity. That sounded like a made-up stage name to him. He was about to ask her, then changed his mind. It didn't really matter what she called herself, or if she was traveling with a damn circus—like the ones he'd seen back East. He didn't want to get to know her or let her get to know him. He just needed to keep her alive and under wraps until tomorrow.

But first, he thought in resignation, he needed to come up with a plan for tonight. He knew the other men would expect to hear some noise coming from his room. They were probably lined up on the stairs by now, waiting for the moaning, groaning, and heavy breathing to begin. Better not disappoint them. And besides, who knew where a little playacting could lead?

He pulled off his boots and unbuckled his holster. Setting the revolver aside, he crossed the room and sat on the bed.

Trinity dropped the now empty plate, lurched away from him, and crawled to the far side of the bed.

Scrambling after her from behind, Jesse hooked one arm around her waist and wrestled her close to his chest. "It's just pretend," he reassured. "The men are listening, and they'll expect me to be after you all night long." He nuzzled the nape of her neck. "Let's give them a good show."

She didn't move nor make a sound.

"Well say something," he demanded.

"Help! Somebody help me pleeease."

His ears rang with the sudden explosion of pitch and resonance. She sounded dead serious and was a better actress than he'd given her credit for.

"That was terrific. Keep going." He leaned over her shoulder and pressed his cheek against hers. "Come on," he encouraged. "Pretend you're Evangeline and you've just found Gabriel. Although I always thought the ending much too sad."

Bandana still in place, she twisted in his arms nearly facing him. "Evangeline?"

"Well think of a different book or a play. Maybe Shakespeare. Or you'd make a good Mabel from the Pirates of Penzance." He'd seen the play in New York City a mere few months ago. It seemed like years had passed since then. "It was sad that the hero was indentured."

"Indentured…" She struggled harder as if she feared the word as much as him.

"Well if you can't play the part, at least play the game. For an actress, you're not exactly good at pretending."

He glanced down. Her dress was bunched up beneath her, revealing long, shapely legs—all the way to mid-thigh. Suddenly, revenge and playacting weren't the only things on his mind. He reached out—then snatched his hand away.

The last thing he needed in his life right now was a woman—and the last thing she probably needed in her life was a man like him.

Chapter Two

The musky scent of man, leather, and trail-dust drifted over Trinity, triggering a response in her body that left her unsettled and confused. Pushing the odd reaction aside, she tried to keep a sane thought inside her head. Which was more than she could say for the man holding her prisoner. He must be a lunatic.

Being deprived of her sight left her feeling naked and helpless. If only he'd remove the blindfold. And why did this bandit mention Evangeline? Did he mean the poem? Her friend, Etta, had read her the sad tale, but Trinity knew nothing about playacting or pirates. He'd mention indentured though. She knew what that meant...but he couldn't possibly know.

Afraid to move, she recalled his dark, somber eyes and brooding expression. He hadn't looked loco. But he'd told his bandit brothers he would kill her tomorrow. It wasn't fair. She'd done nothing wrong. She didn't want to die, especially not now. Not when for the first time in her life she had her freedom.

Maybe she could reason with him, change his mind. But he'd warned her to do as she was told and not challenge his word—and she'd been trained all her life to obey without question.

"Let's get this over with. I could use some sleep tonight." She jumped at the sound of his voice. "Might as well get comfortable while we're doing it." He stretched out beside her.

Doing what? There might be a great deal more to worry about tonight than the possibility of being shot dead come morning. But she wasn't going down without a fight. Claws unsheathed, she shoved at him, venting her fear and anger. Then her stomach went all queasy, rejecting the food she'd eaten too quickly. Rolling to one side, she moaned and tried not to upchuck on the bed.

"That's more like it," he said with enthusiasm, "only louder."

Was he glad she was sick? Maybe if she threw-up, he would leave her alone.

He bounced up and down on the mattress. The springs and bed frame creaked and groaned, and her stomach heaved all the more. Scared and sick, one hand gripping her stomach, she lay on her side, curled up in a ball with her back to him.

"This sure would be easier if you'd help." He careened to a halt, rolling sideways up against her. His hand rested flat on her hip, and his warm breath tickled her neck. "If you need artistic inspiration, I'd sure be happy to oblige."

Heaven help her, he really was insane.

Without warning, he pressed his lips to the nape of her neck, his touch soft and beguiling. The brief contact sent a wave of sensation shooting though her, but not fear or nausea—pleasure. She reached for the blindfold, had to see him, had to know where to strike to defend her body from his touch—and her mind from the emotions that touching kindled.

"No, no," he scolded, grabbing her wrist. "Keep it on, or I'll tie you to the bed."

The prospect of being restrained brought another round of remembered suffering. She'd been eight years old when her adopted brothers had tied her up and left her in the corn crib overnight. But she wasn't a child anymore—or helpless. Lips curled into a snarl, she struck out as if fending off the rats and spiders that had crawled all over her that night long ago.

"Gees. Settle down. You're close to overacting again. You must be new to the limelight."

Sidelined by his words, she hesitated as Jesse rolled onto his back and bounced up and down again. The bed jumped so hard it hopped along the floorboards until she thought it might drop through to the room below.

"Oh darlin', don't stop. You're driving me wild."

She made one more attempt to scramble from the bed. He grabbed her, crushing her in a bear hug, his mouth by her ear, and his voice low. "You really are a temptation."

His words took her by surprise as he held her tight. He wasn't hurting her. Didn't really seem angry. He nipped at her neck, and the stubble of his beard scraped over her skin, the action more tingly than scratchy. "Damn me for a fool, Trinity. I really do want you." This time his words had him sounding more helpless than she felt.

Deep inside, the slow-burn she'd felt before grew hotter by the minute. She must be scared senseless because her mind was floating out of control like when she'd had the fever. She didn't think he was playacting anymore.

He kissed her cheek, her neck. "We could write an ending to this little drama to satisfy all our needs. A masterpiece worthy of accolades. Come on, you must have kissed men onstage during one of your performances—show me."

There he went again, implying she was an experienced woman. But she wasn't. The increasing desire he displayed suddenly frightened her—she was in over her head. "Please, I'm begging you. I'm not who or what you think I am. And I don't know anyone named Solomon. Why are you doing this to me? Stop, please, stop. I've never been with a man."

He stopped moving and held her so close she could hardly breathe. With her cheek jammed up against his chest, she heard his heartbeat racing wild and fast. After a few deep breaths, he abruptly released her as if he couldn't get away from her fast enough. She heard his feet hit the floor as the rickety bed rocked off balance. A thud echoed through the room. It sounded like a fist hitting a wall.

"Holy hell."

She pictured him cradling his hand. Now he did sound angry, and she wasn't sure why.

Wood scraped against wood as he dragged a piece of furniture across the room. "That was real good, baby," he shouted, "let's do it again." Muffled hoots and distorted yahoos echoed from beyond the door. The other outlaws really had been listening.

As he moved about the room, she inched her twisted skirt down over her thighs and waited and waited, but nothing happened. The last of his warmth and the excitement he stirred ebbed from her body, and for one desolate moment she wished he would come back to bed and hold her. Nothing more, just hold her— even if it was just for a moment. Was that such a terrible thing to wish for?

Alone in her little sphere of darkness, she groped at the bed cover and dragged what she could up over her body. Although she fought hard to stay awake, apprehension gave way to exhaustion.

****

Her eyes snapped open. Was it nighttime? She couldn't tell with this damn blindfold on. Staying absolutely still, Trinity listened carefully, straining to hear what she could not see.

Rain whipped against the roof almost drowning out the grating noise of a man's rasping snores. He was asleep. She sat up and tugged the bandana down around her neck, blinking against the glare of lamp light he'd left burning. As her eyes adjusted to the brightness, she glanced around the room. He was sprawled in a chair in front of the door, his long legs splayed out before him, his hands layered atop his stomach. A hot blush enveloped her, and she recalled the feel of his lanky, hard body next to hers.

With his head tilted back and to one side, shadows accentuated his strong jaw and chin. His cheeks were angular, but not sharp, and his nose was just short of being hawkish. Did a smile twitch upon his lips—lips that had touched her? Dragging her gaze from his face, she studied the rest of the room.

The hatbox Etta had given her sat on the dresser, the lid askew as if he'd looked inside. A towering wardrobe, shoved up against the window, effectively crushed any hope of escape by that means. A dull glimmer of light seep in around the edges—morning must be nigh. She dreaded to think what the day might bring.

Her situation appeared grim. The outlaw sat in front of the door, leaving the only way out around him—and the pistol he now wore.

Swinging her legs over the side of the bed, she glanced down. The front of her dress gapped open exposing more than just a little cleavage. He'd looked at her...seen her. It hadn't seemed real when she'd been unable to see him. Yanking the fabric into place, she buttoned the offending bodice.

Gaining her feet, she headed across the room, sending the hardwood floor into an unholy rendition of snaps and creaks. The outlaw stirred and rolled his head to the other side, but he continued sleeping. She took another step with the same horrendous results.

Eyes closed, the man holding her captive jerked his hand to the butt of his revolver. "Dammit, I told you I'd take care of her come morning." His voice, harsh with anger, sounded as if he meant every word.

Trinity leaped back onto the bed. Would he really kill her? From what she knew of life, the answer was yes. Her attempt at independence had been short-lived, and now she'd have to pay the price for such a daring move.

"Oh, Etta," she whispered. "The cost of freedom might be higher than we imagined."

****

Irritated by such a show of weakness, Etta Mathews swiped at the tears on her cheeks. Then she convinced herself she could be sentimental on her birthday if she darn well pleased. After all, living for sixty-five years ought to afford a body some rights and special privileges.

Drawing her shawl closer against the chilly

predawn air, she rocked faster. Heading inside made sense, and she should check on the bread rising by the stove, but today she wouldn't be dictated to by anyone or anything—especially not the weather. Her morning ritual was to sit on the front porch and watch the sunrise, and that's exactly what she intended to do.

"We'll be all right." She gave a nod of affirmation "And so will she." The words were more to reassure herself than Lord Byron, the Bluetick hound curled at her feet.

The wind blew and the chair creaked, and her gaze settled on the handmade card in her lap. Trinity, God bless her, hadn't forgotten the promise to always remember her birthday. And Etta would never forget Trinity—her wayward, rebellious angel.

The girl had only been gone a few days, but it felt longer. If only there had been another way to save Trinity. But with any luck, running away to Denver would put an end to the unprovoked beatings—or possibly something much worse looming in her future—another type of abuse.

The first twenty years of Trinity's life sure had been fraught with suffering. Twenty years! Yet it seemed like only yesterday she had come into Etta's life. The little girl in the apple tree. That's how Etta would always think of her, even though Trinity had grown up to become a strong and smart young woman.

Born during a furious snowstorm, just this side of Middle Kiowa, the child seemed to have been destined for danger and hardship. Her mother, a destitute woman, ill with fever, had been found curled up on the doorstep of the Holy Trinity Orphan Asylum. Half frozen, the mother died giving birth, and no one claimed to be the father of the poor babe. On that sorrowful Tuesday morning, the nuns at the orphanage had christened the baby girl Trinity Tuesday.

Then, with good intentions, they fostered the babe to Etta's nearest neighbors, the Hatfields. Uneducated ruffians, with two boys of their own, the family made Trinity's life a living hell of servitude.

But Etta believed the good Lord put Trinity on the farm next to hers for a reason. All through the years, she'd done her best to keep an eye on Trinity, offering her sanctuary and shelter as she taught the young girl to read and write and stand up for herself.

With a smile, Etta reread the card Trinity had secreted away in the flour bin. Etta's birthday fell on a Friday this year, the day she always baked bread, so Trinity knew she'd find the note first thing on her special day. Quick of mind and with a big heart, and despite being brought up in a home without love or encouragement, Trinity had a kindness about her.

But make no mistake—she wasn't all sugar and spice. Trinity was a spitfire of a girl, and heaven help anyone who got in her way. Heaven help them indeed.

Chapter Three

Jesse settled his gun belt and holster around his hips as he gave a quick gaze eastward. Last night's rain had finally eased up, and the sun peeked through the leftover clouds on the horizon.

"Stop balking at every turn." He guided Trinity toward the barn, still angry at the both of them for the mess they were in. "The sooner we're out of here the better."

Trinity stumbled along at his side, the hatbox she toted crashing into his leg with each step she took. A tear trickled from beneath the bandana blindfold, leaving a clean path on her dirty cheek. Tears were the last thing he'd expected from the woman who'd dared to land a right cross on his jaw while he was holding a gun on her.

"Will you please uncover my eyes? I promise I'll be good."

"That's a very convincing performance, but I don't believe you, and it's a little late. We needed your theatrical skill last night."

Except for lighting a fire in him, and putting his body in an uproar, she hadn't been much help convincing the other outlaws they were going at it last night. One time, she'd seemed to respond to his kisses. But when he'd proceeded with enthusiasm, she'd gone stiff with fright, asking him to stop in no uncertain terms, and he knew she wasn't putting on a show for the boys. That sure had taken the wind out of his sails and the bulge out of his pants

Digging in her heels, she attempted to wrench away from him. "I don't know who you think I am, and I don't know what you want. And most of all, I don't want to die." Her voice broke on the last words.

He jerked her forward. "What are you talking about? Nobody's going to kill you."

This woman sure had a knack for misunderstanding everything he said. He'd be glad to be rid of her.

Reaching the third horse stall on the right, he took the hatbox, set it aside, and settled her hands on the wooden rail. "Stay put."

He bridled and saddled his horse, counting his lucky stars Old Thomas appeared to still be asleep. Sliding his rifle into the scabbard on Webster's saddle, he led the animal over to where Trinity waited. The gelding snorted and shied to one side. "Easy, boy. It's all right," he crooned, grabbing the reins. "She spooks me too." He tied the hatbox on where his bedroll usually went. "Get on up."

She used her hands with the fingers splayed to blindly feel her way along the side of the horse. "Grab some mane. You ride in front again." Hands around her waist, he boosted her on board to straddle his poor horse's withers. She squealed in alarm, nearly kicking poor Webster in the head. Quickly righting herself, she locked onto his mane with a death grip. Jesse swung up into the saddle and then gathered her onto his lap. Even though she was small, two in the saddle was a tight, uncomfortable fit.

Exiting the barn, he studied the house. Convinced

no prying eyes watched, he headed out at a decent pace while the rest of the men slept off their long night of drinking and bedding the women who had shown up there a few days ago.

At the bottom of the hill, out of sight of the ranch house, his shoulders sagged with relief. He'd pulled it off. The woman hadn't seen anyone else's face, nor had she learned the way to the hideout. She couldn't accidentally betray herself or him.

Should he remove her blindfold? He reached for the knot securing the fabric, then clenched his hand into a fist. She was hard enough to handle without the use of those blue eyes. Convincing himself it was for the best, he disregarded the sad, downcast angle of her head and lowered his hand back to his side.

The morning breeze shifted, drenching him in Trinity's fragrance, sending fractured memories switch-backing through his mind. He recalled the warmth of her body on the bed and the taste of her skin. Desire he'd ignored for far too long had been resurrected. Then guilt pricked at him like a burr in a blanket, but he wasn't sure why. He could have sworn she had enjoyed herself too, at least for a little while. So what if he'd tried to have a little fun with her? She was an actress, wasn't she? He'd assumed she was an experienced woman.

He flexed his left hand—his fist still hurt. Slamming it into the wall had been stupid, but at the time he'd needed something to take his mind off of her silky skin and warm thighs.

Turning his face toward the sun, he tried blinding himself to the images in his brain.

No use getting all riled up over some slip of a

female. He had enough worries to occupy his mind, and the only thing he should be doing with his body was trying to keep it in one piece.

Yawning, he ran the same hand across his face. Dang if he wasn't tired, and not just from last night's short, uncomfortable sleep. He was tired of it all. Who knew keeping up this subterfuge would be so exhausting—as well as dangerous? But he couldn't, wouldn't, give up.

The woman shifted about as if getting restless. Against his better judgment, he loosened and slid the bandana free. She cringed at the sunlight, then rubbed her eyes and glanced around.

"Well, thank you very much," she snapped.

Evidently, she was still in a snit. But then what had he expected—gratitude?

Ignoring her, he tied the blue cloth around his neck and concentrated on the surrounding terrain. The main trail came into view, branching off into three choices. On the left, the well-worn road led to Prairie Ridge. On the right, Stagecoach Road led back east to Middle Kiowa. He urged the roan onto the unmarked center path, a tangle of buffalo grass and skunk cabbage.

"Where are you taking me?"

"You'll know soon enough." He didn't bother to mask the irritation in his voice.

"At the barn you promised to set me free."

"No. I promised not to kill you. Don't give me a reason to change my mind."

She took a breath, the expression in her eyes heating up. He steeled himself for an argument, but she exhaled slowly and remained silent. She learned fast. That was one point in her favor. Besides, she wouldn't have won. Debating was his stock and trade.

He glanced back at the gaudy hatbox. While Trinity slept, he'd taken the liberty of searching through the receptacle. Besides a change of bloomers, he found a book of poems, two letters, and a small sum of money. But it wasn't the right money. It wasn't in the correct denominations, and it wasn't marked. Somehow the plans had changed, and nobody had bothered to let him know.

Asking Trinity questions hadn't gotten him anywhere this morning, so he decided to forego the aggravation of resuming his interrogation. She was either stubborn as the day was long or truly unaware of what was going on.

Guess he'd know soon enough. Dropping her off at the stage office in town sounded risky for the both of them, so he'd decided to sneak her in the backway. Let Sol figure out what the heck to do with her. That image put a smile on his lips.

Studying her mass of tempting blonde hair, he regretted all the more what he planned to do next. Should he explain what he had in mind? Probably not. Like any woman, she'd fight the idea, even if it was for her own survival.

Reaching a stand of cottonwood, he guided the horse off the trail. The nearby stream had turned into a rushing torrent, liable to get considerably worse if another rainstorm hit.

"Whoa, Webster."

Trinity stiffened and glanced around. "Why are we stopping here?"

He swung down from the saddle. "There's a matter that needs tending before we get you back to Prairie

Ridge."

Not giving her time to resist, he pulled her from the horse and toward the water's edge. Then he widened his stance and drew the Bowie knife from his belt scabbard. "We need to do something about your hair."

She stood stock-still, like a frightened deer, eyes wide, the color of a winter sky—that rare shade of blue that melts snow and promises the warmth of spring. Then as if coming to her senses, she made a break for it. He blocked the attempt. She turned and ran in the opposite direction. Only one step behind her, he grabbed a hold of that easily recognizable hair. She stumbled, landing on her knees. Still gripping her hair in his free hand, he gritted his teeth and slashed the blade sideways.

****

Trinity screamed and collapsed on the ground.

Why didn't she feel any pain? Maybe she was already dead.

She squinted open her eyes. The moist earth, only an inch from her nose, looked and smelled like normal sand, rock, and grass. Levering upright into a sitting position, she glanced at the outlaw. Knife in hand, he loomed over her, his expression somber. Sunlight glinted off the well-honed blade he held with casual familiarity. He couldn't have missed.

Then she noticed the hank of blonde hair dangling from his other hand. She jerked her hands up to her head. He'd cut off her hair. He'd been lying to her. He was going to kill her after all. This was probably some weird ritual he performed as a prelude to murder.

When he sheathed the wicked looking knife, she scrambled to her feet, blinking back the tears burning in her eyes. If she was going to die, she'd go out fighting not crying.

"You damnable son of a bitch." She balled her hands into fists ready to let fly with everything she had. "You couldn't just slit my throat and be done with it— you had to play another of your sick games first."

One hand braced on her shoulder, he held her at bay with his outstretched arm. "You are the most excitable female I've ever come across." With the other hand, he stuffed the fistful of hair into the pocket of his vest.

"I'll show you excitable." She maneuvered around and kicked him in the shins.

He loosed his grip on her shoulder and hopped around on one foot. She caught him a lucky blow square in the stomach. The air whooshed from his lungs. Taking advantage of his distraction, she ran toward the horse. The horse ran toward his master.

"Now just let me explain." He grabbed Webster's reins.

"Explain what," she shrieked. The horse snorted and sidestepped. "I've been robbed and kidnapped and sheared like a sheep. And last night in bed..." She paused, unable to find words for the riot of emotions he'd kindled—emotions still smoldering like embers best tamped down.

He arched a brow. "And last night in bed what?" A cocky smile eased across his mouth. "Well?"

Her cheeks burned. He had touched her, and kissed her, and looked at her in places the sun had never even seen.

"You—you know what."

He turned Webster loose, and took a step closer. "I

think you found some of it to your liking."

"I most certainly did not." Could he tell she was lying?

"You didn't like it when I did this?" Resting his hands on her shoulders, he held her in place, kissing her neck below her left ear.

"No."

"Or this." He brushed his lips across hers.

"No." This time, the word came out barely a whisper.

Slipping his arms around her waist, he jerked her closer. His gaze never left her face as her hips collided with his. It was happening again. He was turning her body to liquid fire.

"Liar." He lowered his arms—and stepped back.

She almost crumpled to the ground. His sudden release left her so confused she'd almost forgotten why she was mad at him—until a breeze tickled the back of her bare neck.

"Why in heaven's name did you cut off my hair?"

His mocking smile faded, and his expression hardened. "I did it because you can't go traipsing around Prairie Ridge with your blonde hair waving like a flag. If the boys go into town and recognize you, you'll wind up dead for real. They might be crazy good-for-nothin's, but they're not stupid."

"I can take care of myself. At least I was doing all right before you showed up."

"I sincerely doubt that, and I'm not happy about crossing paths with you either. Just keep in mind, next to drinking and robbing what these men do best is cover their trail. They never leave witnesses." A fleeting expression of pain haunted his eyes. "If it comes down

29

to your life or theirs, you'll lose. Even a face as pretty as yours won't wring pity from these black-hearted scavengers."

Trinity knew she should be frightened by his warning, but the only thing that made an impression on her was that he thought she was pretty.

No man had ever said that to her before. The Hatfield boys had tried to get under her skirts, but that didn't mean they found her attractive. They would have tried to look at her underpinnings had she been ugly as a frog. But Jesse had said the words out loud.

Tucking the feeling away between her other thoughts, she watched him unroll another bandana, this one red. Why was the center black? Mystified, she stepped closer. Jessie grabbed her in a head lock like her horrid stepbrothers used to do, and before she could break the hold, he rubbed her head with the cloth.

Once she was free, Trinity stumbled sideways.

"It's just lampblack—soot from the kerosene lamp in my bedroom. Wait a few minutes before you rinse the soot out in the stream. Be careful you don't fall in."

With a yowl of anger and frustration, she ran for the water. Reaching a little side pool, she knelt and dowsed her head. The shock of cold almost froze the blistering thoughts of retaliation in her mind.

Rinsing out as much of the black as possible, she gained her feet, smoothing what hair she had left back from her brow. Before she headed his way, she bent and filled her hands with sand, mud, and small pebbles and flung all three at his head.

He momentarily turned aside and hunched one shoulder to ward off her attack, the rocks and dirt bouncing harmlessly off his back. "It'll grow out soon enough. Besides, you look truly appealing with dark hair."

"You idiot. You nightmare on horseback. I'll never forgive you for this."

"I'm not looking for forgiveness."

Seething with fury and shivering with cold, she headed for the horse, seeking dry clothing. Then she stopped short remembering there weren't any. Her tattered suitcase was probably sitting in Denver. That was his fault too.

She didn't have the warm shawl Etta had knitted for her, nor one clean outfit to her name. And now her head probably resembled a Holstein cow. She sputtered illogically, too angry to form proper words.

"Here." Now naked to the waist, Jesse held his shirt in his hand, extending it toward her. "Go ahead. You'd better dry off."

Having no other option, she snatched the garment from his hand, and rubbed it over her face and shoulders. The soft cotton smelled like him.

As she dried her hair, she peeked from beneath the fabric. Brawny and tanned, Jesse flexed his muscles as he stood taller and folded his arms across his chest. He seemed completely at ease standing half-naked before her. The unexpected feeling the sight of him stirred deep inside of her was another reason she should be afraid of him.

Once she finished staring at the obstinate man and drying off, Trinity threw the shirt in his direction, hoping the black streaks now marking the front were permanent.

He wrestled the shirt on, taking his own sweet time to button, tuck it inside his jeans, and roll back the sleeves. Adding his vest, he angled his head to one side, scrutinizing her from head to toe. She felt like a brood mare up for bid.

"Not even your own mother would recognize you now."

Having no real mother, the statement held little importance for her other than sadness, but his words did give her pause. By changing her appearance, Jesse may have unwittingly done her a favor. She would welcome assistance from the devil himself if it would help her to evade the Hatfield family. Still, it was a rotten thing to do to her.

Jesse nodded toward Webster. "Let's go. We've got a long ride ahead of us."

Holding her wet skirt high, she stomped the rest of the way over to the horse. "You owe me a new set of clothes. And a handmade shawl. And a ticket to Denver."

He untied the hatbox from the back of the saddle and slipped the bow over the saddle horn. Then he swung up into the saddle. "The only thing I owe you is safe passage back to Prairie Ridge. Get on board."

This time he dragged her up behind him to straddle the horse at his back. With her nose pressed up against his still damp shirt, about all she could see were his broad shoulders. Rangy and tall, Jesse presented a deceptively lanky appearance until one huddled in his shadow.

Without warning, he nudged the horse into a canter. She jerked backward with a yelp of surprise. Off balance, she grabbed his gun belt to keep from falling. Her gaze locked onto the revolver and the row of cartridges held neatly along the leather. Defiance boiled up again, and for one rebellious moment she considered making a play for the weapon. But she had little experience with handguns, and even if she managed to seize his pistol what would she do, force this outlaw to take her where he already said they were going?

Leave well enough alone, she told herself. At least for now.

Shifting her gaze, she studied Jesse's free hand resting on his thigh. Were his hands calloused? What had they felt like skimming across her bare skin? At the time she'd only noticed their strength and the way her body reacted to them.

She snuggled closer seeking warmth, or so she told herself as she flattened her bosom against his back. He made a growly noise and sat up straighter, kicking the roan into a gallop.

Chapter Four

Around high noon, they veered to the right and entered a stand of trees. Trinity welcomed the shade and seclusion, but not the flies and low hanging branches.

Between the tree trunks she caught glimpses of Prairie Ridge. At first glance, the town seemed to mirror Middle Kiowa, only larger. But when the stage had stopped here yesterday morning to take on passengers, she'd been struck by the unusual quiet—almost a haunting solitude. Not a sleepy contented calm, but rather a nervous fearful silence, as if folks were waiting for something to happen—something bad.

Circling around, they skirted the last row of buildings on the eastern perimeter of civilization. A solitary dog rummaged in a junk pile accumulated behind one of the backdoors. At the rear entrance of a two-story house, they eased to a halt. Grasping Jesse's proffered arm, she slid to the ground and rubbed life into her backside. Jesse dismounted too and tied up the horse.

"Whose house is this?" Damp, hungry, and chilled to the bone she decided who lived here might be less important than whether or not they were in residence.

Ignoring her question, Jesse retrieved the hatbox, grabbed her elbow, and hustled her toward the backdoor.

She snatched her arm from his grip and glanced around. This would be a good time to make a run for it. But to where? To the sheriff—if Prairie Ridge had one. And if so, announcing her presence to a law-dog didn't sound like the best of ideas.

She jumped as Jesse pounded his fist on the well-worn wood. "Hurry, Sol," he muttered, and knocked again.

The door opened a crack, and an old man peered out. "Jesse. Come in. Come in." Stepping back to accommodate them he opened the door wider.

Hand at the small of her back, Jesse nudged her through the opening and into the mudroom.

The man's weathered features slipped from surprised to worried as he glanced up and down the alleyway. "What in heaven's name are you doing here, Jesse?" He closed the door and jammed the bolt into place.

"I'm returning the parcel you put on the stage."

Brow furrowed, the old man produced a pair of wire-rimmed spectacles from the pocket of his white shirt. Adjusting the glasses on his nose, he studied her from head to toe.

She instinctively reached to smooth the wrinkles out of her crumpled dress. Then glancing down, she abandoned the absurd idea.

As if her appearance was normal, and all the people he met had horrible haircuts and dirt stained clothes, he politely extended his hand. "I'm Solomon. And you are?"

This must be the man Jesse kept insisting she must know. Instinctively responding to Sol's gesture, she noted his grasp was warm and reassuring, his expression one of amusement rather than judgment. "I'm Trinity." Having already told Jesse her first name, she supposed there was no point in lying to this man.

Jesse seemed about to speak, but Solomon cut him off. "Looks like the two of you could use a cup of coffee." He led the way down the hall to the kitchen. Jesse ambled in the same direction, leaving her to follow.

She glanced back toward the door. There was still time to run, but coffee sounded good. And her curiosity was piqued. Jesse's friend seemed a nice man and appeared to be about the same age as Etta.

"I'll be with you in a minute." Sol busied himself at the stove.

Jesse hurled the hatbox onto a nearby sideboard and slouched down into a chair. He seemed perfectly at home here.

Ready to take flight should the need arise, Trinity perched on the edge of the hardwood seat across from him. Sol seemed a bit old to be a stage robber. Maybe he was the leader of the gang. But then why wasn't he at the hideout with the rest of the outlaws? And why would Jesse bring her to him after going to so much trouble to save her from the other men?

Placing three cups of steaming coffee and a plate of honey cake before them, the older man sat too.

"What in Hades is going on, Sol?"

"I was about to ask you the same thing." Sol took a swallow of the dark brew. "But I didn't think you'd want to discuss business in front of company."

Jesse frowned, and for the first time since she'd met him, he seemed unsure of himself. "I thought you sent her to me, and you'd instructed her on what to do."

"Whatever fostered that concept?"

"The hatbox of course." He nodded over his shoulder at the conglomeration of ribbon and lace looming at his back.

Sol gained his feet and took note of the box. "Well I'll be a monkey's uncle." Then he left the room and returned with another one, almost a twin to Trinity's.

"Aw, hellfire." Jesse covered his face with his hands as if he could make Sol and the hatbox disappear. "I can't believe there are two of those things." He lowered his hands and glanced from one to the other.

"Me neither," Sol agreed, setting the duplicate beside Trinity's.

Trinity had always thought Etta's old hatbox a one of a kind too.

"What happened to the girl you were supposed to send?" Jesse toyed with his cup of coffee, then took a big swallow.

"She fell down, hurting her wrist and ankle, just before getting on the stage. I didn't have time to make new arrangements, and I thought you'd figure out the plan had changed when neither she nor the hatbox showed up amongst the passengers."

Finally, some answers. Jesse had mistaken her for another woman. One with a hatbox like hers. That explained his mysterious behavior, but it didn't excuse what he'd done to her.

"You mean you've put me through all this, including cutting off my hair and dying it black, because of a failed plan the two of you cooked up?"

Sol stared at her head. "Jesse did that?"

"How could you possibly think I would do this to myself?"

"The boy mostly depends on his brains," Sol defended. "He never was too good with his hands." Trinity's stomach tightened. From what she'd felt of Jesse's hands he did just fine in using them. A smile pulled at Jesse's mouth, and she swore the same thought crossed his mind. Just the idea of him thinking that way made her mad enough to spit.

"All right, all right," Jesse began. "I made a mistake. I'm sorry. But I had no choice about your hair, and I can't help it if the stage company is now in possession of your suitcase."

"I don't care whose fault it is. You owe me a new wardrobe and a hat to cover the hideous mess you've made of my hair. I demand restitution." She scrambled to her feet, the back of her knees crashing into the seat, sending the chair scraping backward.

Jesse jumped up to face her. "It seemed like the right thing to do at the time. And you're alive, aren't you. There's been no permanent damage done except to your vanity."

She reached up and touched the stubby ends of her hair. "What a cruel thing to say."

Her kidnapper's mouth flattened into a scowl, and he appeared sorrier than he sounded. He was also handsome and pensive and appeared sincere. Of course, she suspected most outlaws had a gift for lying and for projecting images contrary to their true feelings—if he was an outlaw. Why would a stage robber have a friend in town or care whether or not she lived or died? From the very beginning, Jesse had acted the stalwart hero rather than the villain. On the other hand, he'd certainly ruined all her plans.

"I still hold you accountable. This has been one of

the most horrible experiences of my entire life." Which of course was not true. She'd endured years of worse treatment from the Hatfields.

"Well, I didn't exactly enjoy dragging you around the county while I tried to prevent the other men in the gang from getting their hands on you."

Sol backed away from the table. "I'll just let the two of you work this out between yourselves. Don't get hot headed and leave before I have a chance to say good-bye, Jesse." He gave a chuckle as he disappeared out the kitchen doorway.

Trinity slumped back down onto her chair.

Jesse's scowl darkened as he resumed his place across from her. "I truly am sorry about what happened. I give you my word."

"The word of a bandit. How reassuring."

"No," he corrected, "the word of a man."

She studied him closely. "Why should I believe you?"

His jaw tensed. "I don't know. Maybe just because you want to."

Eyes downcast, Trinity fidgeted with the edge of the tablecloth. She had rarely done anything just because she'd wanted to. Her life had been governed by other peoples' wishes and demands, leaving her little experience at making her own decisions.

Just look at the choices she'd dared to make so far. Running away from home had been her decision. And now not running when she had the chance was also her call. Would either notion prove a wise idea?

"Again, I'm sorry."

Jesse seemed anxious for her to accept his apology. Feeling too tired to keep arguing, she relented.

"Apology accepted."

Warmth replaced the regret in his eyes, and for a heartbeat she felt as if she were looking at someone she'd never met before. A different man. A different Jesse.

"Good." He slapped the table with the flat of one hand, as if sealing a deal or ending a dispute. "Now I gotta get out of here." Up on his feet, he liberated the sheaf of papers from her hatbox where he must have hidden them during the night.

"Sol," he called, setting them on the counter, "where's the money?"

Sol returned to the kitchen and rummaged around beneath the logs in the woodbox. "Here." Excavating a canvas pouch, he loosened the drawstring. A surprisingly large wad of money was revealed.

Jesse reached into his back pocket retrieving money of his own. "This is my share of yesterday's take." He exchanged the unlawfully gained denominations for the same amount of bills which Sol had produced. Then he held one up to the meager afternoon sunlight. "You did an excellent job marking them." He refolded and shoved the new money back into his pocket.

"What about the documents?" Sol gathered them off the kitchen counter.

"I guess just keep them with what I've already given you. Relaying everything to the governor's men in Denver will have to wait." He glanced at her as if the delay was her fault. "But if things turn bad, it's up to you to see all this information gets delivered as we discussed."

"I'll take care of it. Don't worry," Sol promised.

"I'm sorry about the confusion with the courier." He clutched the handwritten records to his chest with one hand and clamped the other on Jesse's shoulder. "Have you got time for some food?" When Jesse shook his head, the older man spoke up again. "Watch your back, son. It's a dangerous game you're playing."

"I know, but until this matter is settled, neither one of us will rest easy." He glanced around the kitchen, as if committing it to memory or reliving an old one. "It's hard telling when I'll be back. Just expect me when you see me."

While continuing to converse, the men turned in unison and headed down the hall toward the backdoor and waiting horse.

He couldn't just leave. The thought of Jesse walking out the door and never seeing him again gave her an odd sense of loss. She jumped up and hurried from the kitchen. For the last twenty-four hours, escaping this man's clutches had been her only concern. Now, desperate to keep him in view a little longer, she rushed on. Considering all they'd been through together, wasn't he going to say good-bye? Then again, why should he? Other than being a nuisance, he apparently found her of little consequence.

Jesse paused at the door, slid back the bolt, and reached for the brass knob. Without knowing why, she prayed he would look back. She wanted to see his face one more time, if only to reclaim her good sense—those lost somewhere in the depths of his sad, dark eyes.

Unknotting the blue bandana from around his neck, he turned and step closer, tying the scarf around her head. "Good-bye, sweet Trinity." He grazed the back of his knuckles along the curve of her cheek, and a heady, reckless feeling set her heart to beating faster.

Then he was gone.

As the door shut, the latch clicked softly into place with the finality of a gunshot.

She stared at the wooden panel separating her from the outlaw who had turned her world upside down. She barely knew Jesse, shouldn't feel anything for him. The fact that she did angered her. Obviously, suffering through the robbery, the kidnapping, and the ruination of her hair had left her unhinged. Now with Jesse gone she'd be fine.

"Miss Trinity, you look a might pale. Are you ill?"

Ill? No, not ill, just drop-dead lonesome. How odd, because growing up fighting desolation on a daily basis she'd become accustomed to the bleak, hollow feeling. But Jesse's absence seemed a different kind of lonesome. One new to her. One even worse.

"You need a good helping of my famous stew and another cup of coffee." Sol led her back to the kitchen and settled her into a chair. Then he went about preparing the food. "Everything will work out. He'll be back."

Irritation replaced her loneliness. Why should she care if Jesse ever returned? Besides, tomorrow she would continue on her journey to Denver, to freedom, to a new life.

Exhausted, Trinity stared at the food before her. Finally, like a clockwork doll, she dipped her spoon into the bowl and raised it to her mouth, over and over. When the bowl was empty, she didn't remember chewing or swallowing or enjoying a single bite.

"Want to tell me what happened?" Sol asked, ladling out more stew.

Trinity studied Sol. Although dark like Jesse's, his eyes somehow inspired trust and confidence. Again, she thought of dear Etta, and before she knew it, the details of the stage holdup and her kidnapping were tumbling from her lips.

"And then we came here." She fell silent, and shaking with cold she gave in to the overwhelming fatigue now returned full bore.

Sol patted her arm. "I think you're in shock, little lady. And who could blame you after what you've been through? You need hot water for washing up, a hot toddy, and a good rest."

"Is there a boarding house nearby?" Her voice sounded as weak as she felt.

"Not really. Prairie Ridge could use a good one. There is what passes for a hotel, but it's a might expensive by most folks' reckoning. There are rooms, of course, to let temporarily over the saloon. But I wouldn't advise either place. You're more than welcome to stay here."

She hesitated.

"I insist, Miss Trinity." His voice was firm but not harsh. "Jesse's my nephew, and since he caused your dilemma it's only fitting that someone in the family makes amends for your inconvenience."

Sol was Jesse's uncle—there was a surprise. She shouldn't trust a stranger, especially one related to an outlaw, but she had little money to spend on a hotel. Besides, Solomon seemed a nice old man. She liked his name. It was the same as the wise king in the Bible. And she liked the way he called her Miss Trinity.

"Yes, all right. Thank you."

He smiled and led her up the stairs to the second

floor and a sleeping chamber. "You wait here. I'll be right back."

The room was clean, tidy, and orderly—except for the large stacks of books piled randomly on the desk in the corner. A mustache cup and mahogany comb and brush set proclaimed it a man's room. There were two big windows letting in muted light. One faced a big tree, the branches nearly touching the house. What would it have been like growing up in such a wonderful room?

Sol returned with her hatbox and a bundle of clothes.

"What's that?" She eyed the fabric and lace.

"Only a few old dresses." There was a catch in his voice as he set them on the bed. "I've a feeling they'll fit you just right, although the styling may be a bit out of date." He lingered, his fingertips hovering over the clothes. Then he clenched his hand into a fist. "I'll bring the hot water and the toddy."

She wandered over to one of the windows. The distant rolling hills were haloed in burnished gold as the afternoon sun headed toward the horizon, and more clouds were building in the west. It was later than she thought. Hand pressed flat against the pane of glass, she sighed. Why did the world always seem brighter just beyond her grasp?

Maybe everybody felt that way—even Jesse. Was he back at his hideout? The thunderclouds had grown darker, even a bit sinister in the direction he'd headed. She hoped he made it back without a problem. She didn't understand why she wanted him to stay safe, but she did. And almost like an omen, the clouds chose that moment to block out the sun.

Pretending not to care, she inspected the stack of clothing. Lace edged the collar and cuffs of the dress lying on top. The dress was soft and clean, and the buttons were made of real pearl. She laid the dress aside and reached for another and another and another. Each item of clothing seemed more expensive than the last. All of them nicer than any Trinity had ever worn. Some nicer than any she had ever seen.

Who had they belonged to? One of Jesse's lady friends? Her fingers curled into the fabric. What if he were married? She hadn't even considered that possibility. Indignation burned on her cheeks, and her hackles rose. For no darn good reason, she was jealous. She couldn't remember ever feeling that way before. The emotion didn't set well with her.

Then she pictured Jesse with a mean, shrewish wife and a wagon full of kids. That would serve him right. But he'd seemed unencumbered, the only thing on his mind his furtive plans, which did not seem to be going well.

The last article of clothing, a nightgown, was heaven to touch. Pure white and ethereal, it seemed woven from moon-glow. The bodice, embroidered netting, dipped in a provocative style, and the long, full sleeves ended in points of lace. Tiny rows of tucking cinched the waist, and yards of diaphanous cotton billowed to the floor.

Clasping the gown to her bosom, she waltzed across the room. Expectations of appearing as beautiful as the gown ran high until she paused before the mirror. Startled by her reflection, her grip slackened, and the lacy fabric slipped through her fingers. Her cheeks and chin were streaked with dirt, and the tip of her nose was sunburned. She snatched the bandana from her head. Her hair stuck out in spikes and twists, while patches of black marked her scalp. She really did look like a curly-haired Holstein.

Tears threatened. How had Sol been able to keep a straight face? No wonder he'd left the bottle of cleaning solution when he brought the dresses. It wasn't for her clothes—it was for her hair.

Throwing the bandana on the floor beside the dressing gown, she stalked back and forth the length of the room. She couldn't go to Denver or anywhere else looking like this. For heaven's sake, when on the run, one tried to blend in with the surroundings not stick out like a corn stalk in a wheat field.

She snatched up the nightdress and wadded it into a ball. She hated Jesse. By mistake or not, he'd ruined more than her hair. Her plans for the future were falling apart as quickly as his plans for those papers.

Ashamed for taking her anger out on the nightdress, she shook out the wrinkles and draped it over a chair. Even if Jesse wasn't particularly cruel or mean, she hated him on general principle. He was cocky and arrogant. He also knew Shakespeare and stories about pirates. That gave her pause, and her temper cooled a few degrees.

Nearly every room in Etta's small house held books. And the older woman had read and loaned many of them to Trinity. But how could a brazen outlaw be acquainted with such literature? The idea seemed ludicrous. Although she had to admit, tired as she was and with the evening nigh and bordering on the realm of dreams, such a fanciful notion seemed rather romantic.

Sol gave a little cough announcing his presence. She turned toward the door. He stood in the threshold, teakettle in one hand, a hot toddy in the other.

"Oh, I didn't hear you. I must have been daydreaming."

"Nothing wrong with that. It's good for the soul." He set the kettle on the floor near the washstand and the toddy on the little table beside the bed. "There's the usual facility out back and a chamber pot under the bed."

He wandered over to the chair where the white nightgown glowed brightly even in the dimming light. "She never got to wear this. It belonged to my wife," he added, a catch in his throat.

"Why did she never get to wear such a lovely garment?" As soon as the words were out of her mouth, she regretted invading Sol's privacy.

He didn't seem offended, but his smile seemed wistful. "I ordered it for her birthday from a fancy place back East. She died before delivery. I forgot all about the present until the day it arrived. I didn't know the garment was mixed in with the others."

Trinity gathered the gauzy white array and pressed the soft bundle into his hands. "You'd best take it for safe keeping."

He gave a little nod, handling the material gently. "There's cheese and bread in the larder if you get hungry. Otherwise, rest well. I'll be around if you need anything."

She sank down onto the edge of the bed. Everyone had their own story to tell, and it seemed each held a large measure of heartache.

With a sigh, she watched the final glory of the day

fade to darkness. A moment of peace. The first one in quite some time. Then thunder crashed and lightning stabbed across the sky. With a shiver, she reached for the hot toddy.

The good never lasted.

****

The storm that had followed him back to the hideout continued to rage, and the hour grew late. Jesse wished Billy Bart would hurry up so he could go to bed.

The leader of the gang inspected Jesse's revolver, rotating the cylinder to check the load, then smelling the tip of the barrel. "Don't lie to me, Jesse. You been gone a long time, and your pistol ain't been fired today."

Not bothering to struggle against the two men who restrained him, Jesse stared the man straight in the eye. "I never said I shot her, Billy. I slit her throat."

The other man's gaze flickered.

"After I had my fill of her again. No one to hear her screamin' out where I took her." His stomach churned at the grisly image his own words conjured, but the only way to survive around men like these was to be as badass or worse than they were—or at least to pretend to be.

Billy slid the Bowie knife from Jesse's belt scabbard. The blade was stained with dried blood. On the way into Prairie Ridge, Jesse had noticed a fresh coyote kill just off the trail. Now he thanked God he'd had the foresight to stop on the way back to the hideout to dip the knife in what was left of the dead jackrabbit.

"And what's this?" Billy pricked at Jesse's vest pocket with the tip of the blade.

Trinity's hair lay nestled inside. He'd been foolish

to keep it. Was his sentimental lapse in judgment about to trip him up? "Just a keepsake. She sure didn't need it anymore."

Billy freed the swatch of curls. "You're a sick bastard, Jesse. But you got style." He nodded toward the two men. "Let him go."

They released Jesse and clapped him on the back. Two seconds ago, they had doubted his loyalty. Now they acted as if they admired him for the grim tale he'd just told. They were less than animals.

He studied their faces, wondering if he'd ever know which one of them had killed Jacob. Revenge knotted like a fist in his chest. But he fought back the rage, stopping himself from coming out swinging. Soon...

Billy slapped the knife handle and lock of hair into Jesse's outstretched hand. "You were lucky only the girl seen you during the hold up. You better be more damn careful in the future."

By the look in the other man's eyes Jesse knew he was treading on thin ice. "Sure thing, boss." He stuffed the hair back in his pocket, returned the knife to its sheath, and retrieved his revolver from the table. Out of habit, he checked the load before holstering the weapon.

"I'm for bed. That little filly plum wore me out." Casually, he threw the marked money Sol had given him onto the sideboard with the rest of the stagecoach loot. "My share of yesterday's take." Not waiting for comment, or slowing his step, he headed for his room.

Reaching the sanctuary, Jesse removed his hat, gun belt, and spurs and flopped down onto the bed. Although his plan had gone off the rails, things hadn't turned out too badly. At least they were both alive, and the woman was safe. The best laid schemes o' mice an' men.

He raked his fingers through his hair. He sure could use a good night's sleep, but while physically exhausted, his mind kept running full tilt. He stared up at the watermark on the ceiling and a blurry image of Trinity formed in his mind.

Was it only last night they had shared this room—this bed? He shifted his head on the pillow and inhaled. Her faint powdery smell lingered.

How could he have made such a stupid mistake? She could have been killed, and it would have been his fault. Revenge was a dangerous master to follow. Devoid of compassion, it offered no concession to bystanders while exacting a high, nonnegotiable price.

Up until yesterday Jesse hadn't cared much about little things like that. If he didn't watch out, he could end up as hard-hearted as the man he pretended to be. Or hurt someone in his rush for justice. Someone like Trinity.

He eased the coil of blonde hair from his pocket. Pulling a thread from his frayed shirt he tied off one end. Then he braided the silky length like he did the ends of his lariat. She sure had been a handful—in more ways than one.

Knowing Sol would watch over her until she left on the stage, he wondered if she was nestled in his old room. In the bed he slept in whenever he sneaked into town? Knowing she might be left him unsettled.

He closed his eyes and recalled how she looked this morning by the stream—her hair slicked back, her face scrubbed clean, the wet dress clinging to the front of her body. He still felt badly about her hair. But he'd been telling the truth when he'd proclaimed she was attractive regardless of the length or color of her hair.

Ruing such foolishness, he opened his eyes, rolled to the edge of the mattress, and sat up. Tugging off his boots, he tossed them across the room purposely hitting the wall with two resounding thuds. He wished he could go back to when he never knew she existed.

Standing in the dark room, he shrugged out of his clothes and crawled naked under the covers. Then he willed his mind to ponder other matters—like how he was going to take down Mr. Briggs and help clean up the town. All-consuming thoughts—until he tucked the braid of hair beneath his pillow. Then he was lost again to the memory of a woman he hardly knew. And he felt restless as a wild cat, and lonelier than a rogue wolf.

Chapter Five

After last night's heavy downpour, the morning sun was much appreciated. The light filtered through the lace curtain, creating pretty patterns on the bedroom floor.

Wearing a plain cotton nightshift, she'd found among the dresses, Trinity sat on the edge of the bed studying the room in greater detail.

While she was growing up, her attic bedroom had been drafty in the winter and stifling in the summer. To peek out the one small window, she'd had to stand on a chair. Still the dreary room had been her private domain, the only bit of the world she could call her own. Now even that was gone. Nothing belonged to her, and she belonged to no one. It was more freedom than she'd bargained for.

After washing in the leftover chilly water, she quickly donned one of the dresses, and yielding to temptation, she wandered about the room. Had Jesse slept here, maybe even hoped and dreamed here. Had he been his true self here, the person he seemed determined to hide—just as she hid her true self.

Opening the top drawer of the dresser, she unearthed an oval tintype. A smiling, youthful version of Sol stared back at her—a dark-eyed beauty clung to his arm wearing one of the dresses Sol had brought to her.

Carefully replacing the tintype, she retrieved a small wooden trunk with a rounded top. Jesse's reference to pirates came to mind. This war chest held a jumble of curious items a small boy would treasure. Top honors were claimed by a misshapen silver dollar that appeared to have been left on a railroad track and run over by a train. Next came a tooth from some large animal—a bear or mountain lion. A chipped and battered tin soldier lay off to one side, patiently awaiting the next call to duty, and a handful of brightly colored stamps were wedged in a corner.

At the very bottom rested a packet of photographs.

Returning to the edge of the bed, she eased the parcel free and set the trunk aside. The picture on top was a young boy, bordering on angelic, yet with the makings of Jesse's current cocky smile. What had happened to destroy the wide-eyed innocence and trust? She hadn't missed the anger and sadness reflected in his eyes, not cruel eyes, but hard eyes, sometimes cold.

The second photo portrayed Jesse beside a distinguished man and woman. His parents? They looked happy. The third composite included a second child. A brother? Trinity turned the picture over. Jesse and Jacob, ages ten and six. She stared at the inscription. Jesse not only had parents, but a brother also. He'd been loved.

What terrible incident occurred to harden him and make him prefer the company of no-account bandits?

Shuffling through the last few pictures, she noticed the man and woman never appeared again, only the boys, and Sol. But one thing was constant in all the photos. In every pose the two boys stood side by side with Jesse's arm across his brother's shoulder. Both of them grinning as if they could not be defeated as long as they faced life together.

She traced her finger across their smiles. The concept of a loving family was beyond her imagining. No one had ever given a hoot about what happened to her—except for Etta. And now she was miles away. And one mile or one thousand, it didn't matter. She had to succeed and make it on her own. If for no other reason than to make Etta proud.

Envisioning Etta rocking on the porch brought her solace. She was sure to have found the birthday card by now. Regardless of where she ended up, Trinity had promised to never forget Etta's birthday. Maybe next year they would celebrate together in Denver.

Etta had talked about selling up her property and moving closer to her cousin in the big city. With the escalating wars between ranchers and farmers, things were not as peaceful as they once were on the prairie. Whatever the future held for either one of them, there was no turning back.

What would Etta think of Jesse? His name had come to her last night in a dream. The sound echoing from afar as if captured by the moonlight and whispered on the wind. Haunting her, daring her to remember the wanting his touch had sparked in her body. From that, too, there could be no turning back. Thoughts of Jesse caused an ache both painful and divine, and she reckoned only his return would make it go away.

But how silly and weak-willed to pine for an outlaw. She should forget him, although running into Jesse felt like a turning point in her life, as if it were meant to be. Perhaps Etta had been correct when she said good or bad things happen for a purpose.

Trinity hadn't believed it until now. Until she'd met a man who made her feel as if she hadn't been running away at all, but rather she had been running toward something.

A rumbling and thumping filled the air, the noise more horrendous than the thunder and lightning last night, and dropping the collection of photographs, she leapt to her feet. Rushing from the room and down the stairs, she headed toward the front of the house, following the rhythmic clack, clack, clack whirring noise growing louder step by step.

Reaching a set of large oak-paneled doors, she paused. Whatever the monstrous thing was, it waited on the other side. Bracing herself, she reached for the brass knobs and flung wide the doors.

Sol stood at the far end of the room, facing a hodgepodge of belts, rollers, and pulleys. The apparatus before him moved in all directions at once, yet it didn't move anywhere at all. He gave the attached wheel a turn and pumped the foot pedal. The muffled thumps and clanks assaulted her ears with new vigor.

She drew closer. When Sol didn't react, she reached out and tapped him on the shoulder.

He spun around and then slumped in relief. "Young lady, you scared two years of life out of me, and at my age I can't afford to be doing that too often." Although he seemed to be shouting, his words could hardly be heard.

He was quite the sight. The sleeves of his white shirt were rolled up, and elastic garters gripped the fabric around his upper arms. A once-brown apron, now stained near completely black, covered him from chest to knees.

The contraption ground to a reluctant halt and a welcoming silence blanketed the room, "She's a beauty, isn't she?" Sol nodded over his shoulder, and proudly slipping his thumbs beneath his suspenders, he rocked back and forth on his heels a few times.

"It's wonderful," she agreed, "but what is it?"

"Why it's a printing machine." He lowered his arms. "An Anglo-American Arab. A bit of a mess when I got her, but now she runs like new. Don't mind the mangled parts." A precisely cut piece of wood bolstered the metal leg on the far side, keeping the contraption nearly level, while the flat plate in front showed obvious hammer marks.

Trinity glanced about the room. A tower of cut paper sat on the floor. The smell of machine oil and India ink permeated the air. Against a nearby wall stood a large wooden cabinet with what seemed like a hundred tiny drawers.

"Can you read?" Like a curious owl, Sol peered at her over his spectacles.

"Oh yes. Etta saw to that. Reading has kept me sane in my darkest hours."

"Reading can be a great comfort." Sol nodded, tightening a loose bolt on the frame of the press. "Who's Etta?"

"The lady who taught me how to—dream."

Sol straightened and studied her face. "Sounds like Etta's a pretty special person."

A jagged lump of sorrow lodged in Trinity's throat and it hurt to swallow. "Yes. She is. And I miss her terribly."

"Has she passed on?"

"No. But she's awfully far away. I may never see her again. She was the only friend I ever had."

Sol's expression of sympathy deepened.

Trinity glanced away. She didn't want pity, and she didn't want to think about Etta anymore. Etta wasn't partial to weakness, nor to people who fell prey to what she considered a flaw.

"Your hair's a bit more appealing today."

The change of subjects had her cringing, and she smoothed a wayward tendril along her cheek and neck. She'd left her room on the run, forgetting to wear the bandana. But although her hair remained mottled, at least her scalp was back to its normal color. "Thank you. The mineral spirits you brought helped."

"Good." Sol stepped closer to the spoked wheel, setting the mechanical beast back into action. His movements were smooth and without hesitation, as if he'd performed each task a thousand times before. The machine responded like an old friend who remembered the same dance steps, and amidst all the noise and fury his ritual of work had an almost calming rhythm.

"What are you printing?" she hollered over the din.

"The Prairie Ridge Review." Sol shifted around to face her. "I'm the owner and publisher—as well as the ink roller, the typesetter, and the delivery boy."

Sol's pride for the myriad of titles was obvious, and she had the feeling this profession was his passion.

"Need a job?"

Was he joking? She searched his face for a sign of humor but found none. "I doubt I could be of much help before I leave today for Denver. Might you loan me the dress I'm wearing until I can purchase one there? I promise to send this one back to you."

"Denver? Today?" He appeared confused. "There's no stage coming through today."

"But you don't understand. I can't possibly stay here."

Memories of the Hatfields battered her from the inside out as cold fear lodged in her chest. She must leave. If they caught her before she reached Denver, it would be all over.

Chapter Six

Bored beyond belief, Trinity paced the length of the parlor. Recently, the stage line had dropped their service in Prairie Ridge to once a week. It would have been nice if someone had mentioned the change to the schedule. Now, having been cloistered away at Sol's for nearly five days, she was fit-to-be-tied. Soon she'd be mad as a March hare.

Raised on a farm where the work was never done, she was unfamiliar with leisure time and what to do with so many idle hours in the day. She wasn't very good at sleeping late and had already read nearly every book in the house—even a few of the complicated ones in the room where she slept.

Her eyes were red-rimmed, and her head pounded. There was nothing to do. Even trying on the pretty dresses lost its charm after a while.

Trinity helped around the house and with meals, but she hadn't taken Sol up on his offer of work. The idea seemed too permanent, too normal a step when her situation was anything but. Besides, being around Sol reminded her of Jesse. An odd bittersweet memory at best.

Wistfully, she paused and glanced out the front window, wondering why Jesse hadn't returned, or if he ever would. For some reason she worried about him and knew Sol did too. Once or twice at the hideout she'd gotten the impression Jesse was as much at risk as she, remaining out of necessity rather than choice. Why else would a man like him pursue such danger? Then she wondered why she even cared.

Unable to stay put a moment longer, she edged toward the front door. The raucous sound of the printing press droned at her back. Chances were Sol wouldn't even know she was gone.

Giving in to the thrill of defiance, she tied the blue scarf over her head, snuggled the borrowed shawl closer, and slipped out the door onto the boardwalk. The streets of Prairie Ridge were deserted. During the day, the town slept like the dead. Only after dark did it come alive—with a vengeance. At night she heard rowdy noises coming from the bordello and gambling hall, along with the war whoops of drunken men, and the forced tinkling laughter of hard-working women. On occasion, she'd even heard gun shots.

Reaching the mercantile, she peered through the window. There was only one customer inside, a young woman. That seemed harmless enough.

Entering as unobtrusively as possible, she sidled along the wall, browsing through the bolts of fabric on a table near the door. Sewing made her murderous, usually taking her so long to make repairs on her few dresses she hated the item upon its completion. Still she delighted in the bright hues of silks and the gay patterns of Calcutta cloth.

Stepping nearer to the cash register, she eyed an open bin of mismatched buttons. Fascinated by the splashes of color and glittering copper and gold, she dredged her hand through the bounty, allowing the disks to trickle through her fingers like markers in time.

Where had they all come from? One was of ivory, intricately carved into an elephant. Another held a tiny portrait. Each one so special in its solitary existence. Each one an orphan like her, with no matching companion in form or spirit.

"Your total is thirteen dollars and forty-five cents." She saw the pinch-faced store clerk grab the twenty-dollar coin the girl offered in payment.

"And that's three dollars and fifty-five cents in change."

The man dropped the jumble of change into the young woman's hand. When she hesitated, staring at the money, the shopkeeper shoved the sack of merchandise at her.

"That's six dollars and fifty-five cents change." The words were out of Trinity's mouth before she could stop them. "You've shorted her three dollars."

The clerk's head snapped up, and he glared at Trinity with such ferocity, she took a step back.

"You'd do well to mind your own business, missy," he snapped. Angrily fishing around in the cash drawer, he tossed three more dollars onto the counter.

The girl grabbed the money and headed toward the door.

Having no desire to remain alone with such a disagreeable and unscrupulous man, Trinity followed.

The slim brunette was waiting on the boardwalk "Thank you for what you did back there."

"You're welcome. We women have to stick together."

A peculiar expression shadowed the girl's face. "You're new in town, aren't you? Otherwise you wouldn't have risked causing a rumpus in one of Mr.

Briggs' establishments."

Hesitant to reveal too much about herself, Trinity considered her response. "I'm just passing through. I don't even know who Mr. Briggs is."

"You're better off not knowing him, but you might want to lay low until you leave. By the way, my name's Mary June." She sifted the packages in her arms and looked Trinity up and down. "Prairie Ridge is a rough town, and you don't look like you've had much experience in dealing with the kind of people who drift through here."

Remembering the horrible condition of her hair, Trinity pulled the scarf farther down over her forehead.

"Would you like a cup of tea? I live only a short distance from here."

Trinity's mood brightened. Her desire for company goaded her toward accepting, but the warnings to lay-low everyone kept throwing at her won out. "I guess I'd better not."

"So…you're like the rest, after all." The smile disappeared from Mary June's mouth. "I'm surprised you bothered to help me in the first place."

"Like all the rest of whom?" The woman's abrupt change of mood came as a surprise.

"Like all the rest of the so-called good citizens of this town."

"I declined your offer because you're a stranger, and I don't know who I can trust. What other possible reason could there be?"

"I suppose the fact that I'm one of Mr. Briggs's girls had nothing to do with you saying no."

Trinity was the last person to criticize someone's parentage. "Why should I care who your father is?"

Mary June sputtered, and then burst out laughing. "I'm not his daughter. I'm in his stable of women."

Not sure how to respond to that, Trinity remained silent.

"You know, a soiled dove, a lady of evening. Oh, for heaven's sake, I'm a prostitute."

A prostitute... But she seemed like such a normal young woman.

"What did you expect, horns and a tail?" Mary June gave a wry smile.

Trinity snapped her mouth shut. "I'm sorry. I've never met anyone like...I mean in your line of work."

"Well, now you have. Thank you for your help."

Trinity stared after Mary June as she headed down the boardwalk. What harm could there be in simple cup of tea? Curiosity gained a toehold, and Trinity was lost.

"Mary June," she called, hurrying in the same direction. "My name is Trinity. And if your offer still stands, I accept."

The brunette slowed her steps and smiled. "I have sweet cakes as well."

Question after question streaked through Trinity's mind. Mary June must be a gold mine of information on the subject of men. Maybe she could explain why Jesse's eyes had seemed to say one thing and his words another. Or why the mere thought of him made her feel frightened inside even as she yearned for the adventure he seemed to promise.

Taking a shortcut between two buildings, they reached the back alley. Trinity followed her new acquaintance up the backstairs to the second floor of the brothel. The long hall opened up to show several rooms, the doors closed. At number two-twenty-three,

Mary June paused and pushed open the unlocked door.

The sunny parlor held a sofa, a low table, and two wing-back chairs. Near the window, a wicker cage hung from a stand and housed two small, yellow birds cheerfully twittering and singing.

Through a curtain of Venetian beads Trinity glimpsed a separate alcove. Most of the space was filled by a big brass bed, heaped high with pillows and a comforter. A washstand and basin stood tucked in one corner beside a free-standing mirror. Had Jesse ever been to a place like this? Had he been here?

A hot blush crept into Trinity's cheeks as she imagined Jesse lying naked on the bed, beckoning to her, wanting her. With a cough, she turned away and forced herself to concentrate on the birds.

"Oh my. Aren't they pretty?"

"They're canaries." Mary June stepped closer to the cage and made kissing noises. The birds hopped over, angling their beaks through the bars, touching her pursed lips. "I don't know if they're both girls, both boys, or one of each so I just call them the Lemon Twins. They're such good babies, and they can always charm me out of my sour moods."

Trinity had never dared to have a pet. On the farm it didn't pay to get too close to anything you might be eating the next day.

Mary June stepped away from the birds, and her expression sobered. "Do you know your letters as well as your numbers?"

Surprised by the question, Trinity hesitated. "I can read fairly well." She actually read quite well, but Etta had also taught her not to be prideful. "Why do you ask?"

Mary June scooped up a formal-looking paper from the table and held it out. "I'm supposed to put my mark on this by the end of the month, but I don't know what it says. I was hoping you'd be kind enough to read it to me."

Trinity slid the document, which appeared to be an agreement, from Mary June's hand. "I can't understand some of the words either," Trinity admitted. "But I think it means you owe Mr. Briggs half of all the money you make, with room and board taken from the fifty percent you keep. If you fall short in payments due, he can up his percentage to an even higher rate."

"Oh no, it's even worse than I thought." Mary June's tone sounded hopeless.

"What if you don't sign it?" Trinity handed back the paper.

"Bad things happen to girls who cross Mr. Briggs."

"Bad things?"

"Yes, horrible, bad things." A pained expression sharpened Mary June's features, and her voice trailed off into a whisper. "One girl who worked here held back money a few times. The night her misdeed came to light, we found her in the alley beaten to within an inch of her life. She was so disfigured she couldn't sell her favors anymore. And with no book learnin,' she had no other way of making a living."

Mary June grew silent, a faraway look in her gaze.

Such a revelation came as both a sorrow and an odd comfort to realize there were other people in the world cast off by life. "Is the girl all right now?"

"She's beyond the pain." Mary June's voice wavered. "The rest of us girls tried to help with what little money we could spare, but last Christmas Eve she walked out into a blizzard and froze to death. I guess the holidays were just too much for her. Nobody found her until spring. And she's not the only one to disappear." Anger flamed in Mary June's eyes.

There were times Trinity had felt lonely, scared, hopeless, but at least she'd had Etta. She bet Mary June knew what it felt like to weep alone in the night. Even now her eyes were bright with unshed tears.

"It's long over," the young woman chastised. "There's no need for all this fussing."

"Maybe not. But a good cry never hurts."

"Hell on horseback." Mary June laughed off the sadness. "I should be pouring out our tea, not my woes. I didn't mean to carry on so."

"I don't mind, really."

Mary June stared at her with seeming curiosity. Then she crossed the room to the door. "I'll be right back with the tea. Make yourself at home."

Trinity wandered about the room. A small bookshelf held several well-worn volumes. The Wild Irish Girl, Pickwick Papers, Letters on the Equality of the Sexes and the Condition of Woman, Madame Bovary, A Tale of Two Cities. What an unexpected collection of literature.

"How did you come by all of these books?" Trinity asked as Mary June swept into the room carrying a tray laden with a tea pot, cups, and cakes.

"I bought them along the way as I headed west."

Mary June placed the food on the low table situated between the two overstuffed chairs.

"But if you cannot read..." Not wishing to offend her new friend, Trinity didn't finish the sentence.

"Someday I shall be able to read. It's my fondest

dream."

Trinity knew the importance of dreams. They were the backbone of life, the fragile framework upon which reality hung. The only thing that you could believe in when the rest of the world turned its back on you. They were the difference between giving up and going on.

Following her dream meant Trinity should be in Denver right now. How many years had Mary June been out on her own, surviving in a world that ignored merit and need in favor of cunning and might?

"Have you lived in Prairie Ridge very long?"

Mary June thought a moment then raised her brows in surprise. "Why it's been well over two years. I was only going to stay a few weeks, set some money aside, then move on to San Francisco—or some other place filled with glamor and excitement. But the weeks turned into months, and the months turned into two years." She picked up a cup and sipped her tea. "Don't let that happen to you, Trinity. Never let anything or anyone stand in the way of your happy endings."

"It's never too late," Trinity encouraged.

"I hope you're right," Mary June said, the smile returning to her face. "Someday things will work out for me. Then I'll look back on these times as if they'd happened to somebody else."

You had to admire Mary June's spirit. And for the first time, Trinity truly understood what a precious gift Etta had given her. Because Etta had seen to her education, she had choices in her life. Choices women like Mary June would never have. Too bad Etta couldn't help these girls too, lost in an uncaring world.

Mary June studied Trinity with a critical eye. "The color of your dress certainly suits you," she said politely, "but the styling is a bit old. Camille, one of the other girls working here, lives and breathes the latest fashions from Paris. She's a wizard with a needle and thread. I'm sure she could redesign some clothes for you."

"That sounds wonderful. What a nice idea." Of course, even if Sol would allow the alterations, she wouldn't be in Prairie Ridge long enough to take advantage of such an offer.

Mary June straightened her collar and smoothed a wrinkle from her skirt. "Camille re-fashioned this dress for me last month. Now it's my favorite frock."

"It truly is lovely." Trinity nodded, reaching for another tea cake.

The time slipped away, and a feeling of camaraderie transcended the barrier of their having just met. This is what it was like to have a companion your own age. Gazing again at the bookshelf prompted thoughts of Etta. Was she lonely for someone her own age? She must be, though she'd never mentioned the fact. Why had it never occurred to her that Etta might be lonely too?

Mary June refilled their teacups and settled back into her chair with a sigh and a chuckle. "And then there's men. Can't live with 'em and can't make a livin' without 'em."

Trinity leaned forward in anticipation. She could barely wait to hear what Mary June knew on this subject. Then she felt a nippy breeze as the nearby curtain fluttered in the open window. The warmth of the day had fled. She glanced at the clock and gasped in horror. It was nearly four o'clock. She'd been gone for hours. Sol would be furious.

She leapt to her feet and rushed to the door then paused.

Opened mouthed, Mary June followed on her heels.

"Good-bye, Mary June. I really must go. Thank you for the tea and cake. I hope someday all your dreams come true."

Out the door and through the hall she fled down the steps and onto the backstreets of Prairie Ridge.

****

Sol was waiting at the door, his face pale, his lips flattened into a grim line.

"I'm sorry. I didn't mean to be gone so long."

"You shouldn't have been gone at all. And sorry don't change what's already done." He sounded furious, but at least the color slowly returned to his cheeks.

She stepped over the threshold and waited for Sol to close the door.

He did so with a bang, and before she could apologize further, he stalked past her toward the back of the house.

"I couldn't stay inside a moment longer," she tried to explain, hurrying after him. "I was careful. I didn't mean to make you worry."

Sol stopped short and turned to face her.

She careened to a halt nearly crashing into him.

"I raised two boys in my time. They both turned out good, yet one's dead and the other's robbing stages. I gave up worrying a long time ago."

"One died?" Jesse had known sorrow as well as love. "Jesse's brother?"

Sol's gaze sharpened as if surprised she would be

aware of such information.

"I peeked at the photographs in the dresser up in the bedroom.

"Jacob was his name. He stumbled through the backdoor one dark night, gunshot and covered in blood. We didn't make it much farther than right where you're standing when he collapsed and died in my arms."

Her gaze darted to the floor. Was it her imagination or was the wood discolored as if once stained with something dark? She thought of the pictures of Jesse and Jacob holding hands, sharing a childhood, building joyous memories. To have all that savagely ended must be worse than never knowing such happiness at all.

"Do you know who killed him?"

He shook his head. "And I've said too much already." Sol's expression softened. "It's all right." He patted her shoulder. "Least wise it will be soon as Jesse gets everything straightened out. And for what it's worth, I was worried about you."

"You change moods as swiftly and unexpectedly as your nephew." Her accusation was lighthearted but accurate.

"Maybe it's hereditary." Sol headed toward the kitchen. "Mostly I'm being crotchety because I hate to iron. How are you at doing shirts?"

Terrible, she thought. "Terrific," she lied.

He gave her a sideways glance as if he knew she fibbed. "At least it might keep you out of trouble." Setting the irons on top of the hot cook stove, he left the room, and returned with a large basket of white shirts.

"Heaven help me. Do you iron but once a year?"

"I put on a clean shirt twice a week," he announced proudly.

"But why?"

"Because the newspaper business is not just a job, it's a profession, with high standards and time-honored principles. And besides, I can think better when I'm dressed properly."

Trinity smiled. "Etta had a similar theory about wearing her old Sunday-go-to-meeting hat while she mucks out the barn. Claims it helps her to remember she's a lady even if she's knee-deep in dung."

Sol chuckled. "I think I'd like Etta." Then as if he feared Trinity might renege on her offer to iron, he retreated from the room.

She plucked the first shirt from the basket and took her place behind the ironing board. By true dark, she had nearly finished half the shirts, and she'd only scorched one sleeve and slightly burned two fingers. A remarkable achievement considering her skill level.

The Hatfields regarded ironing and similar affectations a waste of time. If it didn't turn a profit or help to run the farm, it wasn't done. What a welcome change to be around someone who appreciated the niceties of life.

Waiting for the next iron to heat, she gazed out the kitchen window. A nightingale's trill purled through the gathering darkness. Did Jesse appreciate the simple pleasure of a bird's song? Doubting she would see him again, her musing about him seemed an innocent enough pastime. He was miles away, and no longer a threat to her heart—or her virginity. She could live out any fantasy she chose, and unlike real life, the story could have a happy ending.

With a dreamy smile she returned to ironing. Amidst rising clouds of steam, with the fragrance of hot bleached cotton spiraling upward, Tennyson's Lady of Shalott came to mind—her all-time favorite poem. Etta couldn't understand why she liked such a sad story, but it seemed to have been written just for her. A lonely young woman, seeing life through a mirror, never being a part of the real world. Would she risk her life for love?

Medieval images danced through her mind, but instead of a hero in shining armor she saw a reluctant knight in worn leather and Levi's. Setting the iron aside, she crushed the white fabric to her chest pretending the shirt belonged to Jesse, the warmth coming from his embrace. Then she came to her senses, laughing at such foolishness. Now the shirt would have to be ironed again.

Acting in haste had consequences, although she'd hardly call this repenting at leisure.

Chapter Seven

Rain fell day and night as the dreary week finally came to an end. The stage was due any minute, and although she should be excited, an odd sense of reluctance sat heavy upon Trinity's heart.

Clutching her now notorious hatbox, she glanced at Sol. He'd loaned her the little brown suitcase at her feet, as well as the dresses packed inside. "Once I'm settled, I'll be sure and return the traveling case and dresses."

He smiled, but an expression of sadness remained in his eyes. "Maybe someday you can bring the items back in person. Until then consider them a gift."

Only a week ago, Sol had been a stranger—now he seemed like an old friend. He had shown her nothing but kindness, and his witty, intelligent conversation had been the saving grace of her forced occupation. She was going to miss him.

The ticket master rapped on the counter, garnering the attention of all those gathered in the stage office, and a hush fell over the small group.

"Attention, everyone. Attention please." The man behind the counter cleared his throat as if he had something of great importance to tell them. "The bridge on the South Platte betwixt Godfrey's Junction and Prairie Ridge is washed out. There will be no stage coming through today from Middle Kiowa. And the

Bijou river to the west is jumping its boundaries and there's flooding for miles on both sides. So, even if the stage could get through, there's no passage from Prairie Ridge to Denver, unless you know a horse who can swim like a fish."

An uproar of loud voices and a flurry of activity filled the room as the distraught would-be passengers talked amongst themselves.

Trinity didn't move. She barely drew a breath.

"How long will the repairs to the bridge take?" a man standing up front asked.

"Least a week," the stationmaster replied, "maybe two. Won't see no stage 'til then."

As the knot in her belly relaxed, Trinity pretended to be crestfallen.

Sol took up the suitcase and edged closer to the counter. Trinity stuck by his side. "Will this young lady's ticket be good in two weeks?"

"Sure thing," the man in charge reassured. "But if there's another price war with the stage company between now and when you leave, don't be expecting no partial refund."

"No, of course not," Sol acquiesced. "And I won't be expecting any additional charges should the price go up. My niece and I will check back with you periodically."

Trinity glanced up in surprise. Before she could speak, Sol cradled her elbow in his free hand and escorted her out the door.

"We haven't been as careful as we thought. I've had some sideways glances and nosy questions regarding you staying at the house. I hope you don't mind me adopting you?"

His choice of words had to be a coincidence. Sol couldn't possibly know she'd been born an orphan. "I don't mind. Not at all."

As if laughing at the misfortune they had caused, the wind and rain renewed the attack—sending dejected travelers scurrying back to their places of refuge, their footprints leaving new marks in the deepening mud.

Trinity kept pace with Sol as they ran down the boardwalk, the advent of more long days of boredom dogging her heels. She had to find something to occupy her time.

"May I take you up on your offer of employment?" She shouted the question so as to be heard over the drumming of the rain and the clattering of footwear on the slippery, wet boards.

Sol's face brightened. "You'd make a top-notch assistant. We'll get started right away."

****

As he introduced Trinity to the ins and outs of the newspaper business, Sol gave no quarter. Soon her head swam with information about pitch and type and column lengths and lead stories. She set, cut, and hauled paper, and even learned to oil the fly wheel and adjust the belts and pulleys on the temperamental old letter press.

Trinity worked through the morning and afternoon. The humidity made her hair damp and curly, and even with the bodice open a tad and her sleeves rolled up, it was downright hot.

As evening slid into place, they tidied up the print shop area, at least as much as the permanent chaos would allow.

"You might have a glimmer of potential." Sol

untied his leather apron, a big grin on his face.

Although she knew he was kidding, she pegged a handful of type at him. He quickly retreated behind the machine. "What I meant to say was you show incredible aptitude and uncommon intelligence for the job."

"And don't you forget it, mister."

She was having fun—the realization came as a surprise. With Etta, the times they shared were stolen hours mainly spent on learning or reading. Although there was the time in the summer of '85 when the heatwave drove both humans and animals near insane, and she and Etta ended up sitting in the horse trough to cool off. That had been fun indeed. She wished Etta was here.

By nightfall, although ready to drop in her traces, she had to admit the back-breaking work held several gratifying moments. She had helped to create a newspaper. For someone who loved to read, what could be more thrilling?

Exhausted but happy, she crawled into bed.

****

Standing beneath the old oak, Jesse stared up at the bedroom window. It had been a long day, and he rued having to wait until dark to sneak away from the hideout and into town.

Figuring Sol was asleep, he decided to hit the hay and talk to his uncle in the morning. At least tonight the rain had been reduced to a swirling mist. He couldn't remember such a wet spring season.

Gripping the raspy bark of the tree, he sought the familiar niches and handholds while remembered boyhood escapades flashed through his mind. The climb had seemed easier when he was a lad.

High enough now to reach the window, he paused and leaned against a limb to study the horizon and the night sky. Tonight, Prairie Ridge seemed quiet, the town folk having been driven off the streets by the weather and mud. With a deep breath, and a deeper sigh, he welcomed the much-needed moment of peace.

Things sure were changing out at the ranch. The outlaws were becoming even more uncivilized. They were bored, so they drank, which led to fighting and challenging the pecking order. Today, lazy and defiant, the lot of them decided it was too rainy for robbing stages, and they spent the day having their way with the latest assortment of women. These females had just shown up unexpectedly. They seemed frightened and awfully young, speaking mostly in foreign languages.

A few months ago, when he'd first joined the gang, the same thing had happened. Women showed up— then women disappeared. He'd tried to investigate, but again he'd not found the opportunity to single out one of the women to speak to her. He'd spent the day alone in his room, the door barricaded as he reviewed his evidence and wrote up the details. It was time well spent. When the authorities brought Briggs in, he wanted a rock-solid case against the man.

With a yawn, the desire for sleep hit him full force and he raised the second-floor window and scrambled over the sash. In the morning, he'd give Sol the new documents.

Waiting for his eyes to adjust to the darkness, he relaxed his shoulders. The kinks and tight muscles uncoiled, and a calming relief slipped over him. The kind of calm that came from being in a place that sheltered years of memories.

Familiar with the room, he didn't bother lighting a lamp as he placed his hat and gun belt on the cedar chest by the wall. At least now with Trinity gone he could reclaim his lair and good senses, and then get on with trying to balance the scales of justice. She would have left on this morning's stage—yet the fragrance he associated with her seemed to have lingered.

Tugging his shirt off over his head, he dropped it to the floor. Then he leaned against the wall and wrestled off his boots and socks. Unbuttoning his trousers as he crossed to the bed, Jesse shagged out of his pants and slipped under the covers.

The bed felt different, and the mattress out-of-kilter—just like his life. Closing his eyes and breathing deeply, he tried to relax, as if such a state of mind could be achieved while his brother's killer still roamed free.

Then he thought about Trinity. She must be halfway to Denver by now. He recalled lying next to her in bed and wished she were here right now. In sheer folly, he reached out, expecting to find a cold and lonely mattress to match the cold and lonely feelings locked in his heart.

To his great surprise, he touched soft cotton and warm flesh. His eyes flew wide open. Someone else was in the bed. It had to be Trinity, but why was she still here? He sat up and peered through the darkness to no avail. The slight action stirred her, and she sighed, and he wanted nothing more than to take her in his arms.

Resisting the urge, he tried to ease out of the bed. She jerked awake and sprang to her knees. He rose up beside her, clasping her to his chest and clamping one hand over her mouth.

"It's me, Jesse." She went stiff as a dead carp. "I'm going to let you go. Don't call out." He gave her a little shake trying to elicit a response from her. "Do you understand?" He felt her head nod.

As soon as he let go, she vaulted out of the bed. "What are you doing here?" Her voice hit the mark between a screech and a whisper.

"I came to town to speak to Sol." Rolling out of bed he snagged his pants off the floor and turning his back quickly pulled them on. Then he lit a lamp. "It got late, and I decided to wait until morning. I thought you were gone, or I'd have picked a different room in which to pass the night."

Not expecting to see her, he couldn't help but stare at Trinity as if she were some kind of apparition. She wore one of his nightshirts, her short tresses a rebellion of tangles and twists begging to be tamed into submission. "Why are you still in town?"

"The bridge washed out. The stage can't get through from Middle Kiowa. And something about another river flooding, so even if it could make it here, there's no road from Prairie Ridge to Denver."

That surprising bit of news hadn't reached the hideout. Now they were an island in the middle of nowhere—and sending a currier to law enforcement or the governor wouldn't be happening anytime soon. He supposed a man could ride due north or south along the river and eventually find a place to cross, but that could take days. He was really on his own, and if all hell broke loose, he had no backup.

Trinity took a step closer. He edged away. Their last encounter in a bedroom ended with him hot and bothered and her pleading to be left alone. He didn't intend to go through that again.

"Wait." Fingers splayed, she rested both hands upon his chest.

Desire and need returned—like a punch to the gut. Then the hot thrill streaked lower. When she nuzzled her face in the crook of his neck, he levered her away from his chest. "What are you doing?"

"I thought you might be a dream." Her whispered words echoed his previous thought.

He kissed her soft then hard—not missing the little mewling sound she made or the way she sagged against him as if she'd gone weak in the knees.

"Is that real enough for you?"

"Yes. Real and wonderful."

Not the answer he'd expected. During their time apart, had she had been thinking about him too? Of course, if she'd been telling the truth, one thing wasn't likely to have changed. "Are you still claiming to be a virgin?"

"Yes, but no longer by choice."

"What the blazes is that supposed to mean?"

"That day by the stream, when you called me a liar, you were right. I liked the way you made me feel—and I wanted…I want more."

The moonlight broke through the clouds, etching her in a pale glow, reminding him of the innocence lying beneath the brave words. An odd sense of responsibility, or something he couldn't name, had him hesitating as if he were leading her astray.

"Jesse, fate has delivered me to your bed not once, but twice. I don't have the strength nor the desire to resist you a second time."

She blinked her eyes and stifled a little yawn. Was she even fully awake?

Nope. This wasn't gonna happen. He had no intentions of wooing a virgin or dealing with the resulting emotional aftereffects. Now he'd better get out of here pronto because only a saint or a dead man could keep resisting such guileless seduction.

"I always believed the third time's a charm." He gathered what he'd come in with and headed for the bedroom door. "Don't follow me."

Chapter Eight

Another gloomy morning broke to the east. Trinity threw back the covers and sat on the edge of the bed. Had he really been here?

Despite overwhelming desire making her willing to risk all to be with him, she'd done as Jesse demanded and stayed put last night. Was he downstairs in the kitchen waiting for her?

Jumping up, she began to dress. Then she sank back down on the edge of the bed. Why would he hang around in the morning waiting for her to come down? They had met again by accident. And just because he made her feel so alive, so special, didn't mean she was special to him.

She tried to recall what Etta had taught her about the closeness of a man and a woman. Something about it being spiritual, a renewing of the soul, a sharing of minds and expectations.

Those were hardly the feelings she felt for Jesse. And since meeting him, why had her loneliness become even more painful.

As was her usual approach, she fought the aching in her heart with anger, and tugging one of the pretty dresses over her head, she jammed her feet into her shoes. Couldn't he at least just talk to her? Jerking the comb through her tangle of hair, she decided Jesse truly was a bandit, and he'd carelessly stolen her heart, which seemed like the last thing he wanted.

****

Standing just inside the door of Mr. Briggs's office, Jesse waited for the tyrant who ran the town to speak. All hail the emperor, ringed by his gambling hall court, and crowned by a bordello overhead.

"Does Billy Bart know you're here?" Briggs asked from the other side of the polished mahogany desk.

"Nope." Jesse shifted his attention to the man's face. "I only pretend he's the person in charge because he likes it that way, not because I think he's the boss."

Briggs grunted noncommittally and chomped down on the big cigar in his mouth. "Sit down," he growled around the stogie," and tell me what's on your mind."

Jesse took the proffered chair. Briggs was fast becoming one of the richest men in this out-of-the-way corner of Adams County. He was already one of the most ruthless. Not a tall man, whatever he lacked in height he made up for in cunning, arrogance, and cold-blooded disregard for anyone who got in his way.

"You're not getting your money's worth out of me," Jesse began.

Briggs raised a brow and leaned forward. "Meaning what?"

"Meaning, I can do jobs for you that are more complicated and important than robbing stages."

"Such as?"

"Such as keeping the ledger and inventory for you. I'm so good I can keep two sets of books, if you like. A set for you and a set for—other purposes. I can manage the warehouse and oversee the general store selling overpriced sundries to the locals. I can even make this whorehouse start showing a bigger profit."

He could almost see the wheels turning in the greedy man's head. "If you're so all-fired terrific, what are you doing in Prairie Ridge? Why aren't you in Chicago or St. Louis or Denver?"

Jesse smiled. "For the same reason you're not in one of those places. Sometimes the law there can put a cramp in more than a man's style. Then there's only two ways to proceed. You can either stay put and learn to walk with a limp, or you can move on to a place where you can step lively and make your own rules. I favor the latter option, and I think you do too."

Briggs's eyes narrowed. "Why should I trust you?"

"You shouldn't," Jesse said, "and you don't. That's why I'm offering to work for a percentage of the profits. If I fail, I don't get paid."

Briggs stroked his chin in contemplation.

"What about the men I already have doing some of those jobs?"

"Find them something else to do. I'd consolidate their work. Less men, less wages. I'll be able to adjust funds where and when you say they're needed—without hesitation. And there won't be any bickering or infighting in the ranks of management over fair shares or favoritism."

"You'll have a great deal of power at your fingertips," Briggs pointed out.

"Yes, in a way. But you'll still have the final say." Jesse held his ground, and a steady gaze. This had to work. He needed a job on the inside.

Briggs re-lit his cigar and savored three puffs. "If nothing else, you got guts, boy." He tapped the ash into a silver ashtray. "Let's give it a try."

"You won't be sorry."

"If you screw up, you sure as hell will be."

Jesse knew this wasn't an idle threat.

"Now get back to the ranch. I'll need a week to make arrangements here."

"Yes, sir." Jesse gained his feet and turned toward the door. "This means a lot to me, Mr. Briggs," he called over his shoulder. *More than you'll ever know.*

He strode through the gaming hall and out the front door.

Adjusting his Stetson, he allowed himself a brief moment of satisfaction. Although too soon to celebrate, and reckoning the hardest part was yet to come, this was a big step in the right direction.

Leaping into the saddle, he kicked Webster into a gallop. Then with the reckless courage of a man who had seen the elephant and lived to tell the tale, he headed down the middle of Main Street like the devil rode herd on his coat tails.

He thundered past Sol's house and print shop without looking up, and his mouth tightened into a grim line. He wished he'd been able to see Trinity this morning. He didn't want to keep going on alone in the world. He wanted, needed, to share his life with someone. But if the usual pattern of his life held true, when something good happened, something bad followed. Why should this be any different? The ray of sunshine Trinity brought to his life could hardly be expected to dispel a time-honored tradition of darkness.

Last evening had been an altered world, the nighttime world, where for a few minutes he could be the man he wanted to be, and not the outlaw he was forced to be. Trinity might drift out of his life without ever knowing who and what he really was, and that mattered to him.

Bent low, he urged his horse to keep up the breakneck pace. Trees blurred, and the ground hurtled by beneath the hooves of his mount while his emotions ricocheted off into ten different directions.

After Trinity had fallen asleep, he'd stood in the dark outside the door to his old room, wanting more, yet knowing if he went to her, he risked replacing yearning with regret. Then before daybreak, he'd grabbed his clothes and slipped downstairs to see Sol. Sneaking off like a coward before she awakened.

He should have stayed and told Trinity she was special, told her he wanted to see her again. For crying out loud, he should have told her something. But lately he lived on lies and untold truths. That was no way to begin a relationship.

Associating with outlaws made it easy to grow accustomed to deceit. He needed to keep his distance. His plotting and scheming amounted to no more than a house of cards. If that house came crashing down, anybody close to him was liable to get buried in the rubble.

Cresting a hill, Jesse reined Webster into a walk. Last evening, by the light of the moon, being with Trinity had been magical. By the light of day, the concept seemed destined for doom.

Chapter Nine

Trinity hurried down the back alleyway toward the bordello. Questions for Mary June racing through her mind faster than her feet racing down the muddy path. She must have done something wrong for Jesse to cast her aside last night. And for him to leave this morning without even saying good-bye.

At the backstairs, she hiked up the hem of her skirt and took the steps two at a time. Panting to catch her breath, she paused at Mary June's door and knocked.

No answer.

Maybe Mary June had a customer. Trinity hadn't thought of that. Lately, she hadn't thought of a lot of things until it was too late. No use breaking such a sterling record.

She knocked again.

The door creaked open and a bleary-eyed Mary June peeked out through the crack. "What time is it?" she mumbled.

"I'm sorry," Trinity whispered. "Were you asleep?"

"I do work the night shift." Mary June yawned and rubbed her eyes. "But now that I'm up, you might as well come in." Turning, she shuffled to the nearest chair and curled up on the seat. Wrapped in a large robe and scrubbed free of all makeup, she appeared so much younger.

"Are you alone?" Trinity asked, peering around the apartment.

"Of course." Mary June chuckled. "The type of men who frequent here don't stick around once they've had their fun. Nor do they wish to be seen here in daylight."

Jesse hadn't stuck around either. Trinity paced the length of the room.

"Why are you here?" Wariness had crept into Mary June's voice.

Trinity sat on the edge of a vacant chair. "I almost did something terrible. Well not terrible, it could have been wonderful, but the consequences could be terrible, and even though I know I shouldn't do it, I really, truly, wanted to." Jumping up, she stared out the window for a moment then turned back. "I probably shouldn't be bothering you with this."

Mary June nestled a cheroot between her lips, struck a match, and held the flame to the tip. "Settle down." She took a puff and exhaled a billow of smoke. "You wouldn't be the first woman to succumb to a hard body, a handsome face, and a big helping of sweet talk."

"How did you know?"

Mary June just smiled.

"We only kissed. I wanted more, he wanted more, then he just up and left."

"Well maybe next time things will go better," Mary June said with a gleam in her eye.

"I doubt I'll ever know, because he's gone. Without so much as a goodbye."

"How typical." Mary June vigorously tapped the ash off the cheroot into the ashtray. "Is he married?"

"I don't think so."

"A prominent social figure?"

"Hardly."

"Then he's running scared."

"From what?"

"Either your pa, the law, or himself"

Trinity remained silent. She didn't know why Jesse would be running from himself, and she couldn't picture him running from any man, even Pa Hatfield. It had to be the law, which made sense of course. He'd sneaked out early so he wouldn't be seen. Believing the reason had been for his safety made the rejection slightly better. "I thought perhaps he left because I had done something wrong."

"Men are hard to figure at times. Unless you're in bed with them. Then what's on their mind is pretty obvious."

"Not to me."

"When you're together, just do what feels good," Mary June encouraged. "Nothing is taboo if you are both consenting. And you should use a preventative. The last thing you want is to get pregnant."

Actually, that frightful thought had crossed her mind. She reached for the back of the chair. What would she do if she got with child? She'd help to raise the Hatfield boys—the monstrous little pukes—from diapers to long-pants. And when they were old enough, they had turned on her. She wanted none of that.

"There wasn't any need."

"Well the next time there might be."

Trinity shook her head. "He's gone."

"Don't underestimate a lady's power over a man," Mary June reassured.

"But he swooped into my life, filled me with overwhelming desires, and casually rode off into the sunset. Or in this case the sunrise. I'm the one bewitched, not him."

"Maybe. Only time will tell."

Relaxing her white-knuckled grip on the back of the chair, Trinity wandered around the room. Mary June seemed to so easily take things in stride. She should do the same. It wasn't the end of the world after all. If nothing else, she was still better off than she'd been a week ago, a month ago.

Trailing her fingers along the row of books on the shelf, she studied the titles again. "It's awfully nice of you to listen to my woes and to offer your advice." While she was stuck in Prairie Ridge, there must be some way she could repay such kindness. The book titles blurred as an idea came to mind.

"Mary June, I'm going to teach you to read."

Mary June, who had just taken another puff of her cheroot, choked on her inhalation of smoke. Fanning her face, she gained her composure and rose up on her bare feet as if in a trance. "You would do this for me?"

"Yes." Trinity recognized the joy filling Mary June's heart. She'd felt the same way when Etta had promised to teach her.

"And your friends are welcome too," she added, hearing other women's voices in the hallway. "We'll set up a schoolroom in the back of the print shop. We can meet every day or whenever you'd like. It will be hard work, but we'll make it fun."

"I've never minded working hard." Mary June beamed with happiness. "And I'll trade you lesson for lesson," she added, with a twinkle in her eyes. "There's still a cart load of things you need to learn about men."

Not men. Just one man.

Chapter Ten

The week was finally up. Jesse shoved the last of his belongings into saddlebags. The recent batch of women had disappeared a few days ago before he could speak to any of them, and he could hardly wait to take his leave as well.

To Jesse, the gang of robbers seemed like prisoners of the ranch, with freedom the one thing they didn't have and could not buy. And keeping company with these feral brutes was turning his brain to mush. Oh, how he longed for a conversation with someone at least as intelligent as his horse. Webster was a good listener, although not shy about offering an occasional snort of derision.

Sensing movement, Jesse glanced up.

Billy Bart lounged in the doorway of Jesse's room, his expression anything but relaxed. In fact, Billy appeared pissed off. Good. The rest of the house seemed quiet. Apparently, the other outlaws were sleeping in. Nothing new there.

Jesse straightened and draped the leather pouches over his shoulder. He was pleased his new job with Mr. Briggs was a thorn in Billy's side. Moving up in the hierarchy of outlaws already proved advantageous.

"Something I can do for you before I leave?"

Billy clenched and unclenched his fists, a sneer twisting his mouth. "Other than drop dead, I suppose not."

Billy was spoiling for a fight and Jesse was a hairsbreadth away from giving him one.

The other night Billy had bragged about a murder he'd committed, describing the chase and kill like a man recounting a deer hunt. Whether or not Billy referred to Jacob, Jesse didn't know. No doubt a number of people had met untimely ends because of Billy's vicious temper and love for killing—nameless, faceless images all waiting for justice, all sharing space in Billy's malicious mind.

Tight-lipped Jesse shoved past the man he'd come to hate and started down the steps.

"Damn your eyes," Billy snarled. "You think you can just waltz out of here and take that cozy little job in the city that ought to be mine? As far as I'm concerned you still got dues to pay."

Dues…? Jesse slowed down. Dues…? He'd paid in full with the loss of his brother. Not to mention losing the past year of his life as well as his identity.

"Dues are for women's clubs," he called over his shoulder. "But don't get your skirt in a twist. I'm sure Mr. Briggs will eventually find a place for you—once he figures out what you're good for other than shooting off your mouth and your gun."

The stairs creaked. Jesse tightened his hold on the banister and hurried down to the ground level. Dropping his saddlebags, he lunged to the left and spun around, just in time as Billy charged down the steps behind him.

The gratifying pain of a well-landed left hook shot through his knuckles and wrist as his fist connected with Billy's face. Billy staggered, recovered, and rushed Jesse—catching him around the waist. Together they hit the floor with a grunt and a thud. Rolling to opposite sides, they both stumbled to their feet. Restricted by the confines of the foyer, they circled one another like two bears in a pit.

Anger and the desire for retribution surged through Jesse. Did it show in his eyes? Billy hesitated for a split second. Then like a cornered animal, he came out swinging.

Jesse bobbed and weaved, letting Billy wear himself out. His opponent fought as he lived, with desperation and no rational thought. Choosing his opportunities, Jesse landed one solid punch after another. Blood gushed from Billy's nose, and his breath came in gasps and sputters.

He should feel satisfaction or gratification— something, anything. Then he realized Billy had no more brains than the gun he carried. Beating him to a pulp, or even killing him, would always be an empty victory—still a conquest he'd sought for a long time. One last blow put Billy out of his misery. He collapsed on the floor, a heap of questionable humanity, unmoving save for the rise and fall of his chest.

Jesse glanced up the stairway to the second floor. The other men had slept through the entire altercation— a lucky break there. He snagged his saddlebags from the floor and retrieved his hat. "Don't bother to get up, Billy, I'll see myself out." He nudged the door open with his foot and took his leave.

The image of Billy crumpled on the floor dogged him as he rode to town. The savage side of his nature had reared its head—he'd enjoyed Billy's pain and taking away the man's pride. What provided the balance to such a visceral action…intellect? Maybe the tragedy wasn't in knowing the primal edge but in liking it too much. Liking it and going one step beyond the middle ground. He was beginning to wonder how a man knew when he'd gone too far.

****

Briggs tallied the gambling receipts from the night before and stored the take in his safe. Then striding to the center of the room, he clasped his hands at the small of his back and admired the decor. The walls were girded in gleaming wainscoting, shipped all the way from Maine. And the chandelier overhead once lit the captain's quarters on a French pirate ship. Now it all belonged to him. He liked owning things—things and people—especially people. What a glorious feeling of power and control. And selling either commodity had become a profitable side business.

Speaking of which, he needed to replenish the inventory. Once the flood waters receded and the roads were more passable, he'd take another trip south to Pueblo. The smelter plant there attracted immigrants like stink on a cow pie. Not speaking English, they were easy pickings. The last culling of women and men were now on their way north to the mining towns in the mountains—where laws and rules of engagement didn't exist. The men would break their backs hauling ore, and the women, already well used by the boys at the ranch, would be on their backs broken as well.

Lounging behind his desk, he toyed with a diamond-tipped pen. He'd better get more of that crazy cactus juice too. Small doses seemed to make the women more compliant. And in greater amounts, it made both the men and women so loco they forgot about trying to escape.

Between his real estate schemes, the brothel, and selling people into servitude, he was doing a roaring business. And his new manager could funnel any questionable profits through the saloon and warehouse with no one the wiser. Now he had the brains as well as the muscle to facilitate all his plans.

Jesse had shown up at a fortuitous time. Billy Bart, brainless and short-fused, might be good for keeping the men in line, but as for the business end of a transaction, he was useless. And if he could train Jesse to do things his way, there would be no stopping them.

Of course, Jesse would take some watching to see if he was telling the truth or blowing smoke up his ass. And once he'd proven himself, he'd make sure Jesse got involved in enough dirty deals to ensure his unquestionable, irrevocable loyalty.

He smiled and lit a new cigar. There were days Briggs felt like he ruled the world. A world where once his abusive father walked. "Not walking now, are you, old man. You're rotting in the grave I put you in."

Killing his father and getting away with it had been a turning point in his life. The beginning of taking what he wanted—whether he'd earned it or not.

And along with power and money came pleasure. But not with his stable of castoff whores. He was more discerning than that. Which brought to mind the female staying with that meddlesome old newspaper man. His niece, or so the story went. She'd appeared innocent at first. But then he'd seen her thick as thieves with Mary June. She must be of loose morals herself to seek out such company.

He'd watched her bold as you please sitting there

having tea. Yes, he'd seen her. He saw them all. He liked to watch. They didn't know about his viewing holes where he observed the customers satisfying their lust—the creamy female thighs, and the hard-rutting backsides of men, the animal sounds and cries of pleasure, his own frantic breathing.

He stole their passion as well as their privacy.

Chapter Eleven

"Oh, Sol, this is wonderful." Trinity positioned one of the chairs a little closer to the table, then straightened the blackboard hanging slightly off center on the west wall. "Thank you so much."

"This backroom needed a good cleaning anyway. Sorry it took so long." Sol handed her three tattered copies of McGuffey's Reader. "Besides, it's good business sense for a newspaper man to help people learn to read."

She smiled at him. "On occasion, would it hurt you to graciously accept a compliment?"

"Yes, it would. I might grow accustomed to your accolades, and then when you're gone I'd miss such nonsense. Of course, if you'd consider taking root in Prairie Ridge..." His voice trailed off into silence.

Trinity had actually considered the idea. The repairs on the bridge were not going well, the near constant rain hindering progress and destroying work already done. And she hadn't been able to send word back to Etta. But the day of completion would come eventually, and a decision about staying or moving on would need to be made. Logic dictated eluding her guardians and seeking help in a big city like Denver made the most sense. But her heart was not so easily convinced.

"When you leave home, you can lose more than

yourself in the crowd."

The truth of Sol's words hit her hard. It felt as if she'd lost everything of importance when she'd left Etta. Now destiny was asking her to tear herself away from new friends, learning a new craft, and if she left she'd never see Jesse again.

"But this isn't my home." The words, while undeniable, didn't ring true.

"Home is where your heart is, Miss Trinity. It's really not more complicated than that."

Yet it was more complicated. Remaining in a small town, not nearly as far from the Hatfields as she'd planned, could put her entire future in jeopardy. There was not one single person here who would come to her defense if the law showed up. That's why she was trying to reach the attorney in Denver—the one Etta's cousin recommended.

"It's up to you of course."

She clutched the books to her chest. Sol was correct. The decision was all up to her. "At least I'll be here until the bridge is rebuilt."

"Then that will have to do." Sol turned toward the door leading back to the house. "Good luck with your first class."

Pride welled as she set the readers on the table and then studied the room.

For the first time in her solitary existence she was going to make a difference in somebody else's life. Passing on the gift of reading felt like saying thank you to Etta. It was also a more edifying pastime than dwelling on her lusty feelings for Jesse. Not seeing him for over a week caused a new type of lonesomeness. Who knew there were so many different kinds?

A rap on the door to the alley jolted her back to the present. This was it. She hoped she possessed the skill to make this work.

"The door is open."

Mary June strolled in, two girls following hesitantly in her wake.

"Thank you for coming."

"It's us who should be thanking you," Mary June countered, urging the other girls forward. "This here is Laughing Kate and Penny take Annie."

Trinity shook hands with both women. Last names appeared to be a rare commodity in Prairie Ridge, which was probably for the best. "I'm so excited to get started. If you've no objections, I'd like to begin our lessons by teaching you to scribe your names." She stepped to the blackboard and grabbed up the chalk. The three girls followed on her heels like a little flock of geese and peered over her shoulder.

"Regardless of how you come by it," Trinity said, considering her own situation, "your name is the one thing that no one can take from you. You said Penny take Annie, right?"

"Yes." The smallest of the women nodded, setting her curly red hair bouncing as Trinity printed out the first name.

"But what does that mean?" Breaking the boundaries of good manners, Trinity had to ask.

"It's my workin' name. It means a man can have me for a penny."

"But that's not fair. I'm sure you're worth much more than that."

Annie and Kate stifled laughs, and Mary June rolled her eyes.

"Well that's just it," Annie explained. "It sounds cheap, but it isn't 'cause it's by the body part used. Why at a penny per tooth, my mouth alone is worth a fortune." She gave a wide smile. "It's a pay as you go venture, you see, and before he knows it, a gent's run up quite a bill. I never get no complaints mind you."

Startling images flurried through Trinity's mind. What would Jesse be willing to pay for her? She'd give anything for a few more enticing kisses. Gripping the chalk as if it were the lifeline to her sanity, she forced Jesse's image from her mind and added Laughing Kate's and Mary June's names to the board.

"Please, take your seats, ladies." As she faced her students, their eager expressions reinforced her enthusiasm for this venture.

"Oh my," Kate said and laughed. "If I'd known we was going to be called ladies, I'd have worn a corset and such." Her melodious tone would make a lark jealous, and it explained how she got her name.

"A corset. Not me." Annie settled into a chair. "I can't think proper when I'm all cinched in. Why oddly enough it was being straight-laced what got me into our line of business."

Trinity sat across from the three and took the bait. "Whatever do you mean?"

"Well," Annie began, her face a study of serious repose, "that first time, if I'd been unbound and able to breathe free and reason clearly, I never would have said yes...or at least I'd have charged a heck of a lot more."

Again, laughter streaked through the room— genuine laughter, filled with comradery. These three were truly friends.

"You'd better jump in with today's lesson," Mary

June prompted. "Those two can keep the bantering up for hours. Around the brothel, they're the resident entertainment."

"Not anymore." A dewy-eyed expression softened Annie's features. "The new manager has stolen center stage, and he's welcome to it. Along with anything else he has a mind to take."

Kate's mouth curved into a dreamy smile as she toyed with a lock of her long dark hair. "We all want what that big boy's got. But so far, we can't none of us lead him astray for love nor money."

"He's a hard one to figure," Mary June agreed, "but easy to look at. Tall, lean, lanky, and all man. You can see it in his eyes. I don't know how he's holdin' back all that need coursing through that fine body of his."

"He's a quandary," Annie mused, "and smart too. He started a new wage payin' policy for us that's as confusing as a patchwork quilt. It has to do with vests and such."

"Investments," Mary June corrected.

"Investments and such," Annie continued. "At first his idea sounded more cruel than Mr. Briggs's last decree. But the money we give him is making money. He also declared we don't have to work on Sunday—unless we want to. And when one of the girls took sick the other day, he immediately sent for the doctor. Yes indeed, the man's a quandary to be sure."

"Are all men so difficult to understand?" Trinity threw out the question as casually as possible.

"Most of them," Annie claimed. "If they weren't, we'd probably like them even less."

"Are you still lamenting over that man you told me

about?" Mary June spoke up.

The woman was too darn perceptive. Trinity twisted her fingers in her lap, unwilling to admit the truth to herself let alone to these three women.

"You can confide in us," Mary June promised.

She had to tell—or burst. "I think about him all the time, in a most unsettling manner. I cannot eat. And if sleep does come, I dream of him and wake up in such a state I'm all the worse for having even tried to rest. Why, I'm afraid I might be in love."

A heavy silence overtook the room. They probably thought her passion silly. Embarrassed by her schoolgirl confession and their lack of response, Trinity stared at the tabletop. When she finally glanced up, she noticed each of the women had a faraway look in her eyes. She'd been wrong. They didn't mock her—they bled for her. They understood what she was going through.

"First time love can be rough," Mary June agreed with a sigh.

"No other man will ever make you feel the same." Annie nodded.

"And if you let him get away," Kate added, "it'll be his memory that haunts you in the dark hours of a long winter's night."

What if she never saw Jesse again?

Chapter Twelve

Several more days passed with no word from the man who had stolen her heart. But at the moment, Trinity was too happy to care.

A rare bit of midday sun brightened Mary June's room, the canaries trilled happily away, and Trinity modeled her newly reworked dress. Sol had given permission for her to have one of his wife's old garments restyled, and her newest student had done an admirable job.

"You were correct, Mary June. Camille truly is an artist."

"It is my most beautiful creation to date, mademoiselle." Camille waved her hands and arms in accompaniment to her flamboyant French accent. "I have it on good authority all the beautiful girls in Paree are wearing such a fashion this season."

Trinity waltzed around the apartment.

"The blue ribbon is the perfect touch," Mary June added. "It brings out the color of your eyes."

As she wound to a stop, Trinity's smile faltered. Obviously talented, but with no education and stuck in her present type of employment, Camille's abilities went unrecognized, ground beneath the heel of the narrow-minded citizenry. The snooty women in town wouldn't buy a dress from a prostitute.

Most of the women at the bordello fought the same

battle. Hopefully, learning to read would help protect them from people who looked down on them and preyed upon their weaknesses. Teaching kindled Trinity's own fighting spirit, and with each new word her students learned she felt as if she were striking back against all the unfairness in the world.

"Are you sure about the neckline?" Camille asked, fussing with the fabric. "I could remove a bit of lace, enhancing the décolletage."

"No, really it's perfect."

After changing into the dress she'd worn to come and pick up the re-styled garment, Trinity offered the seamstress one of the coins Sol insisted she take in payment for becoming his assistant.

"Oh, I couldn't." Camille pushed her hand away. "I'm happy you are pleased with my work, and I'm excited about becoming one of your students. That is payment enough."

"Thank you, then, and I'm glad you decided to join the group. I'd best go prepare tomorrow's lesson." She turned to face Mary June. "Does attending class twice a week make it too hard for the ladies to get away?"

"No. We're all eager to learn as quickly as possible. In fact," Mary June warned, "Kate and Annie said to inform you they're fixing to challenge you to a spell-off. They've been practicing night and day. They even have lists of words tacked up on the headboard of their beds so work doesn't interfere with their studies."

Trinity gave a sputtering laugh as a wayward image flashed through her mind. She would never again be able to hand out homework assignments with a straight face. "Tell them I'll be ready, and I admire their dedication."

"I will," Mary June promised. "See you in the morning."

New dress in hand, and with a nod to her friends, Trinity slipped out into the hallway. The door closed softly at her back. She stood, holding the fabric close. Her new dress would certainly show off her figure. Too bad Jesse would never see her wearing such a lovely frock.

Where was he? The least he could do was let Sol know everything was okay—although Sol's faith in him never seemed to waver. He kept saying Jesse was doing what had to be done. And she kept suspecting there was more than met the eye where Jesse and the outlaws were concerned.

Oh, the heck with Jesse. Once again admiring her beautiful new dress, she ambled down the hall toward the door leading to the outside stairs.

****

Jesse glanced up and down the alleyway then quickly secured the lock on the storeroom door.

Briggs's inventory checked out clean. Not a crate or barrel tampered with or unaccounted for. Nothing incriminating. He would have to look elsewhere for his evidence—like in Briggs's office.

Climbing the outside stairs to the bordello, he reached for the door at the top just as it burst open. A startled yelp rang in his ears, and he teetered on the edge of the narrow landing.

Grabbing the doorjamb and a hunk of calico, he managed to keep upright. Then a ripping sound filled the air, sending him lurching sideways. To avoid falling down the stairs, he latched onto the idiot causing the catastrophe, and together they stumbled back to the sure footing of the carpeted hallway.

"You darn little fool." Brushing yards of fabric from in front of the person's face, he stared at the woman. Eyes wide, cheeks flushed, Trinity stared back.

Emotions he'd been trying to suppress erupted in a torrent. He tightened his grip, fighting the urge to crush her to his chest, to kiss her, to give himself over to a longing that both scared and excited him.

"Jesse..." She said his name with a tenderness he didn't deserve.

Releasing his hold, he forced himself to a less tempting distance. He'd known Trinity was still in town, but he hadn't expected to find her wandering around up here. Rather a surprising leap from declaring her innocence, to having free run of a whorehouse. His glance slipped beyond her to the hallway. Had anyone seen her come here? Did she do this often?

She stared at the material in her hands, then back at his face. "You seem to have a knack for ruining my dresses."

"You seem to have a knack for being in the wrong place at the wrong time."

"As if you cared."

His concern for her boiled upward into anger. "Why are you here?"

"I don't see how that is any of your business." Her reply was served with a stubborn curl of her lip.

"Well, I'm making it my business. I run this place now."

She recoiled as if shocked by the idea.

"You... How long have you been in town?" Her voice barely rose above a whisper.

Now he was in trouble. He'd kept his distance to

protect her and Sol—at least that's what he told himself. Truth be known, he was trying to protect himself—keeping her out of sight and almost out of mind. "I've been here long enough to know it isn't safe for you here, or anyplace in town."

"But you brought me to Prairie Ridge."

"Only because there was no other choice. And I didn't think you would stay. Or at least when you couldn't leave, I thought you would be smart enough to lay low and not go parading through gambling halls and brothels. Billy Bart and the boys are no strangers here. Had they run into you rather than me, you could be dead right now."

She seemed to consider his words but didn't back down. "Mary June and a few of the other ladies are my friends."

"You'd better get yourself a new set of friends. This is no place for you, and they're not your kind."

"You don't know anything about me, or who is my kind. And that wasn't a particularly nice thing to say."

He admired her gumption in standing up for the women. "I'm sorry. I didn't mean that like it sounded. The girls are goodhearted, and nobody knows better than I how hard life is for them—and what they go through. I'm just trying to scare you off any way I can."

"Too bad, because it isn't going to work. You seem surprisingly at home in this atmosphere."

"That's different."

"Why? Because you're a man?"

"No. I told you, I work here."

"But why?"

He rasped one hand across the back of his neck. He wanted to tell Trinity the truth about why he was living in a bordello and confide what had happened to Jacob. Instead he forced himself to remember the danger she was in—the danger he had put her in. He couldn't afford to be kind or spare her feelings—not and keep her alive.

"Don't come around here anymore." He put as much meanness in his voice as he could muster. The expression on her face made him feel like he'd just kicked a puppy. Then he watched as her anger took hold.

"You've no right to tell me what to do."

I do have the right, he thought, because I care about you. The words slashed deep and painful across his mind as if written with the tip of a saber. But he had to do what was best for Trinity, not what was best for his sorry soul.

She hesitated then laid one hand upon his chest. "Didn't you enjoy those special moments we shared? Don't you want to feel that way again?" Hope seemed to hover around her questions as she waited for his reply.

Her words devastated him. She thought him an outlaw, the manager of a house of ill repute—yet she still wanted him. What a rare thing to be accepted without conditions. He so desperately needed to believe in something pure and honorable rather than in the ugliness of death and revenge. But not yet.

At his silence, she tossed the torn dress at his feet. And shoving past him, she ran back out the door and down the steps. For a fleeting moment the vision of her standing before him stayed on his mind. Then even that cherished reminder slipped away when weighed against how he'd hurt Trinity.

Chapter Thirteen

The next morning, Jesse scowled and paced about the kitchen.

"No. I won't see that she gets it back." Sol tied a knot and clipped the thread. "You'll have to do that yourself." He poked the sewing needle into a pincushion and held the calico out to Jesse.

Fortunate to have coaxed Sol into mending the rent dress seams, Jesse accepted the bundle and figured he'd best not push his luck.

"If you hurry," Sol continued, "you can catch Trinity alone in the backroom before her students arrive."

"Her students?"

"Yes. She's teaching some of your ladies to read and write."

When the heck had all this taken place? He thought he knew what was going on in town, in the saloon. It must be a conspiracy—all the women surrounding him were out to drive him crazy.

Sol gave a little smile, as if he found the situation amusing.

With a sigh, Jesse turned toward the door to the backroom. He wanted to see Trinity, more than he dare admit to anyone, even himself. Yet the idea made him feel as if he'd just agreed to jump off of a cliff. Each time he saw her, it became harder and harder to ignore the voice in his head telling him she was the best thing to ever happen to him.

****

There were six students now, and the list was growing—so was her affection for her new friends. Teaching these women to read made her happy, made her want to get out of bed in the morning, gave her life purpose.

The door to the house opened. Expecting Sol, she smiled and glanced up, but the words *good morning* never reached her lips.

Jesse stood there instead, holding her wadded-up ruined dress, looking like he was clutching the torn pieces of his life in his hands. Expectation and remorse shadowed his expression, reminding her of the first day they had met.

She strangled the urge to tell him nothing mattered except the way he made her feel. But it did matter. He'd been living down the street for weeks and never bothered to come to see her. If they hadn't collided on the stairs yesterday, like two runaway railcars, she wouldn't even have known he was in town.

"I'm sorry about your dress."

"You always seem sorry about something." Her words were harsh, but he didn't retaliate, as if he agreed, and that made her feel all the worse.

"Why are you tormenting me? Why do you tell me to keep my distance one day and visit me the next?"

He set the dress on an old trunk and shoved his hands into his pockets as if he didn't know what to do or say. Didn't know—or didn't trust her with his answer? And why would he. She hadn't confided in him either. Their misgivings and unexpressed emotions stood between them solid as a wall.

"Is there any other particular reason you wanted to see me?" If only he'd say the words she longed to hear.

"I guess not."

Hope died a sudden death. "Then you won't need any particular reason to take your leave."

Turning her back to him, she retrieved one of the books from the table. As she marked the passage to be read that morning, she heard him make his way across the room. When she glanced up, the backdoor to the alley stood open and Jesse was gone—along with another tiny piece of her heart.

Mixed voices came from the same direction, and Mary June appeared at the door. "How is it you know our new boss?" The women drifted in, each taking a seat.

Avoiding the question, Trinity collapsed into a chair across from them. Her cheeks burned hot, and she was sure they were as flushed as they felt.

Mary June leaned forward and studied her more closely. "Is that the man you told us about?"

Trinity nodded.

"Hot and bother," Mary June shrieked. "No wonder you surrendered your heart so easily."

Trinity tried to shush Mary June before she said more, but it was already too late.

Kate and Annie scooted their chairs closer. "You've shared the pillow ticking with our Mr. Smith?" they squealed in unison.

"Was he terrific?"

"What did he look like without his clothes?"

"Was he hung like a bull?"

"Was he as hot as he makes me feel when I see him

swagger past my open door at night?"

"Easy, girls." Mary June came to Trinity's rescue. "They only kissed. Besides, she wouldn't know well hung from ham strung. She's a virgin."

"You needn't reveal such a thing like it was an affliction," Kate defended. "Besides, it's a condition easily changed."

"Didn't you enjoy his kisses?" Annie asked, amazement evident in her voice.

"Of course, I did, but Jesse's barely given me the time of day since."

"He's been awfully busy," Mary June defended. "He's become Mr. Briggs's right hand man."

"I don't care if he's the right-hand man of President Cleveland." But inside, she did care— desperately. It filled her with dread to be reminded Jesse had become more involved with the unscrupulous Mr. Briggs—courting disaster on bended knee, heading for trouble at a full gallop. Yet she refused to believe Jesse was enamored of money and power.

A man who believed in poetry could not be a true mercenary at heart. A man who believed in the magic of moonlight would not honor deceit by the light of day.

"You should join us for the party Sunday afternoon?" Annie invited out of the blue.

"I don't think I should." Jesse's request to stay away rang in the back of her mind.

"But its Mary June's birthday." Kate upped the ante.

Trinity glanced at Mary June. The girl looked confused. Then an expression of enlightenment brightened her face. "Oh, yes, it would mean a lot to me if you would come."

The invitation seemed rather last minute, but an afternoon of fun for whatever reason was beginning to sound too good to ignore. "I suppose I could slip away for a few hours."

"That should be long enough." Annie winked, and Kate lapsed into a round of laughter.

"Come to room 301," Mary June instructed. "Go up the back steps all the way to the third floor. It's the only apartment up there."

"It's the loveliest room of all," Annie said with a sigh, "but not used any more. Too costly to maintain and heat. The room became so expensive to rent the men started complaining that if they were going to spend that much money on a woman they might as well marry her."

"That's right," Kate said. "So now we call it the bridal suite."

Trinity grinned at the absurd idea of a bridal suite in a whorehouse. Then second thoughts chipped away at her bravado. She might run into Jesse there, and it was obvious he didn't want to be anywhere near her. But what about what she wanted?

"What time should I arrive?"

"Two o'clock sharp." Mary June glanced at her friends, and they nodded in agreement.

"Oh, and it's a costume party," Annie said, a gleam in her eye. "Yes, that's it, a costume party. And we shall supply a guise for you to wear. You can put it on when you get there."

Chapter Fourteen

Jesse couldn't breathe, couldn't move, as he watched his little brother being shot down in cold blood. The forty-five-caliber bullet tore a hole in Jacob's chest. A hole so big Jesse could see through to the other side of what seemed like forever. He could see all the things they'd done together, see all the things Jacob would never get to do. He should have been there. He'd been too late. The sound of cruel laughter fueled the already overwhelming feeling of helplessness.

Jesse's eyes snapped open, and he fought his way back to wakefulness. Just another of the nightmares he'd been having of late.

What day was it anyway? Sunday, he remembered, and according to the clock on the bedside stand, well past noon. He had allowed himself the luxury of sleeping late. It hadn't helped. He felt as if he'd spent the night battling his way through a gauntlet of demons.

Throwing the covers aside, he struggled to his feet, and an unsettled feeling sent him pacing about the room. His desire for revenge grew more impatient, never leaving his side. Now the corridors of hell haunted him around the clock, the nighttime having become the wicked handmaiden of the day.

He wrestled on his trousers, jammed his feet into socks and boots, and shucked into his shirt. Flexing the kinks from his shoulders, he tried to recall the last time he'd had a good night's sleep—and couldn't.

And then there was Trinity. Knowing she was just down the street preyed upon his senses. He could feel her, smell her, taste her in the wind. He glanced at the half empty whiskey bottle sitting atop the dresser, a flagrant reminder that drinking her out of his system hadn't been successful.

The other day in the backroom at Sol's he'd nearly taken her into his confidence. But she'd reduced him to a pining clumsy youth, with his brains in his pants and his good sense in his back pocket. She clouded his logic.

Leaving his room, he headed down the hall, not bothering to secure the door. All of the rooms, save one, had the same lock, and all the girls had the same key. It made life a lot simpler. And the honor system worked surprisingly well considering the clientele who visited.

Descending the stairs to the saloon, he shook his head in wonder. Who would have thought he would be living in a brothel? Many a night he'd ached for a woman, and he hadn't missed the seductive glances and provocative stances. But something always stopped him. These women were already being taken advantage of—no use adding his name to the list. Besides, he wanted Trinity.

He glanced at the floral wallpaper covering the walls leading down the steps. Women were like flowers, an unexpected delight. Why, even in the midst of a lonely prairie a pasque flower could suddenly appear. Some flowers and women seemed willing to be plucked and savored with no lament or regret. They rode the wind, anxious to move on, always wanting something more, something different. They were the kind of women Jesse had usually gravitated toward. They were the kind of women he should stick with.

He had a feeling Trinity was different. She was the kind of flower he'd want to keep forever. The kind he'd want to press between the pages of his life.

The moment they'd met she'd piqued his interest. And the night he'd stood in the hall watching her sleep he'd felt peaceful and whole. Hopefully, after he'd vindicated the past, there'd be time to dream about the future.

Wending his way around the ground floor to Briggs's office door, Jesse picked the lock—a skill learned from a well-rounded fellow college student. Opening the door, he stepped inside. According to the bartender, the boss had gone out for a haircut, a shave, and a boot shining. Briggs should be gone for at least half an hour, offering the perfect opportunity for Jesse to find evidence to make them all pay.

As he rifled through Briggs's ostentatious mahogany desk, the mantel clock struck two p.m. Dang. He'd forgotten his three o'clock meeting with Mary June. Figuring he'd better pick up the pace, he jerked open one drawer after another, wondering what Mary June wanted to speak to him about. He had suggested they meet in the parlor, but she had insisted on the third floor in the bridal suite. She'd been adamant—not her usual accommodating self.

Whatever Mary June's purpose, Jesse prayed she didn't have anything prurient in mind. The way he felt today, it wouldn't take much to push him over the edge.

Leaning against the desk, he studied the office and

pondered his next move. The floor safe was locked tight, and so far he'd found nothing of interest stashed anywhere in the room. Then a small vase sitting atop a corner table caught his attention.

Ornate and expensive looking, the feminine object seemed out of place in Briggs's world. Crossing over to the fanciful container, Jesse peered inside. A hint of color caught his eye. When his hand wouldn't fit through the opening, he turned the vase upside down and a little book bound in red leather tumbled out onto the tabletop.

After carefully setting the vase back into position, he flipped through the pages finding a list of dates along with a set of obscure numbers and words. Deciphering the information could take a while. He hesitated, and then slipped the book into his pocket. With any luck, Briggs wouldn't discover the item missing anytime soon.

Glancing at the clock, he decided he had just enough time to grab something to eat before his meeting with Mary June.

His interest piqued by what he had found, he left the office and secured the door. This part of lock picking had taken longer to learn.

****

Trinity knocked at room 301.

Mary June opened the door, and the sound of conversation and laughter spilled out around her. The party must have already begun. Trinity stepped across the threshold, taking in every nuance of the high-ceilinged room.

Red velvet drapes, drawn tight, smothered what little dreary daylight there was—a lavish array of candelabrums was employed to drive away the resulting darkness. Oriental carpets cushioned the thick-legged furniture, and a cheerful fire crackled in the hearth.

But the most dominant feature of the room was a huge four-poster. Adorned in a profusion of white and rigged with a billowing sail of a canopy, the bed stood grandly off to one side promising journeys of seduction and enchantment. What passionate memories had been created there?

Mary June ushered her to the center of the room. "The girls volunteered to get you ready for the costume party."

Trinity's gaze swept their faces. "But why a costume party?"

"Because it's fun. Did you never play dress-up when you were a kid?"

Bemused by the concept, Trinity shook her head. She'd rarely played at all, let alone a game called dress-up.

"Never?" Annie asked.

"Well, its high time you did," Kate insisted.

Now the room hummed with murmurs of excitement.

"We'd better do something with that hair." One girl she'd yet to meet waved a pair of scissors, snipping menacingly at the empty air.

Trinity shrank back.

"Don't worry." Mary June held Trinity in place. "Lolly's an expert with her hands. She's yet to fail taming a bad man or a bad coiffure into submission."

Before Trinity could utter a word, the women rushed at her from all sides.

They stripped off her clothes, then powdered and

perfumed her, applying makeup to her face as the clip, clip, clip of Lolly's scissors rang in her ears.

Realizing she was holding herself as stiff as a railroad tie, Trinity relaxed, pretending she was a rich lady with maids waiting on her hand and foot. How wonderful to feel so special and pampered. When the girls ooh'd and aah'd over her, she even began to feel pretty.

When they fell silent and stepped back in unison, their faces shone with what could only be considered motherly pride. Trinity caught sight of her image in the mirror. A miracle.

A good portion of the black was gone from her hair, and a soft cap of feathery blonde curls framed her face. Along her cheeks and at the nape of her neck wayward tendrils which had escaped Jesse's knife blade and Lolly's scissors coiled whichever way they wished.

Pink silk swathed her hips and legs, and raising the hem revealed tan ankle boots, buttoned up the side and sporting heels. A white corset trimmed in pink ribbons and lace cinched in her waist, encouraging every spare bit of her torso upward, creating a remarkable increase in the depth of her cleavage.

She tried walking in the boots. The fancy heels forced her to walk with a sensual sway, making her feel all languid and flowy. "Once I have the rest of this costume, it will be even more captivating."

Whispers and giggles were the response.

"That's the point of playing dress up," Annie explained. "You wear something daring. Something you'd be afraid to wear in real life."

"What about a mask? Do I at least get a mask?"

Her words trailed off as the girls gathered the

toiletries, put the room in order, and made a mass exit. After the door closed, a trembling silence followed, as if the room held its breath.

Trinity sighed and stroked the embroidered bodice of the corset. She looked absolutely sinful and felt positively divine.

A knocked sounded. Hopefully one of the girls had returned with a shawl or cover-up. With her back to the entrance, she bid them enter. The door creaked opened. Glancing up she viewed the room as a reflection in the mirror—just like the Lady of Shallot did in Trinity's favorite poem.

Except the man looming in the doorway wasn't Lancelot.

Chapter Fifteen

Trinity spun around to face Jesse head-on. "What are you doing here?"

"I live here, remember. What are you doing here? I told you to stay away from this place."

"I'm attending a birthday party."

Her surprise at seeing Jesse quickly became desire, warm as liquid sunshine, leaving her feeling like a flower yearning for the light.

He glanced around the empty room. "Are we early or late?"

"I don't know."

"I think perhaps we're both right on time and Mary June planned this whole surprise."

Whether they'd been tricked or not, Trinity longed for Jesse to say all that really mattered was they were together. But he didn't. He just kept staring at her while silence hung in the air, heavy as the fragrance of honeysuckle on a hot summer night.

Jesse narrowed his gaze, his expression turning dark. "What the heck are you wearing?" His voice, hard as flint, cut to the quick. "I don't need any new girls on the payroll."

Her cheeks grew hot. How could she have forgotten her attire?

Recalling what her friends said about first time love and not letting the moment pass into a lifetime of regret, she ignored his harsh words.

"You don't like my costume?"

His gaze jumped to her face. There was fire in his eyes, but not anger. Now he studied her in the most deliciously slow way—his gaze almost a physical touch. "I never said I didn't like it."

"I could take it off if you prefer." She toyed with the ribbon tied at her waist.

A ragged, guttural noise was his only response before he found his voice. "What I want isn't important." Even now his voice wavered. "Where's Mary June?"

The question took her off guard, and hot jealousy bolted through her. How could he think of another woman when she stood before him so invitingly—with an almost hand-written invitation to do more than just look?

"Mary June? Why?"

"I need to speak with her."

Hurt by his rejection, she headed for the door. "Have a seat. I'll find her for you."

Stalking past, she floundered on the high heeled boots, and bit back a curse.

Jesse reached to steady her, his fingers wrapping around her arm, holding fast. "You sound jealous."

He drew her close, turning her in the circle of his arms. Could he see the hurt in her eyes?

"You are jealous. Aw, hellfire, Trinity."

He sounded as if he'd finally given himself over to some unseen force. She struggled against him. "I thought you wanted Mary June."

"What I really want," he whispered, "is you—only you." He kissed one cheek and nuzzled her neck.

His warm breath danced across her bare shoulder, sending a river of wanting rushing through her. Emotionally, she dove in headfirst, willing the wild current to carry her along.

He levered her away from his chest. A troubled expression veiled his eyes. "I didn't plan this."

"I know."

His shoulders relaxed, and a roguish smile softened his mouth. "Destiny seems to keep bringing us together. But I prefer the touch of your hands to those of Fate's. And like I said before, third time's a charm."

She reeled at the implication. This was a huge step, an irrevocable step, a life altering step. She wanted so desperately to belong to someone—but the wanting and the getting were two entirely different things.

"Why don't we have some wine?" As if he understood her need to catch her breath and think things through, Jesse left her side to uncork a bottle sitting on a nearby table. Filling two small goblets with ruby red liquid, he returned, extending one glass in her direction.

The only spirits she'd ever encountered came from sneaking a taste of Mother Hatfield's apple cider. Although making her a bit woozy, she'd liked it well enough. Surely a sip of wine wouldn't hurt. As she reached for the glass, her stomach grumbled loudly— Mary June had thought of everything except food. To cover her embarrassment, she gave a little laugh and took a larger tasting of wine than planned. Unusually tart, it went straight to her head.

Jesse set his glass aside untouched. Reaching for the one she held, he did the same with hers.

"Care to dance?" He swept her into his arms.

"But there's no music."

"Sure there is, if you listen closely."

She heard the pounding of her heart and the humming of the blood rushing through her veins. She even thought she could hear Jesse's heart in counterpoint to her own. Gliding across the room in Jesse's arms transported her to a place of no worries, no time—only the here and now. She'd never felt so alive. Never felt so reckless.

When he stopped, pleasures to come were reflected in his eyes, and she tried to remember what Mary June told her about being with a man. But her thoughts ran together as if seen through Etta's prized kaleidoscope.

She blinked, trying to focus her vision. Something was wrong. She was falling, with no end in sight. Rushing onward with no way to stop—the feeling exhilarating but frightening. She couldn't breathe. Backing away she reached for the wine and downed what was left in her glass. Jesse still hadn't touched his—she grabbed that too. Why was she so thirsty?

Jesse seized the glass from her hand. "Slow down, Trinity. We've all the time in the world."

Did they? Why did her body feel so heavy, yet her mind light and floating away?

"Is it getting dark? Jesse, I'm having trouble seeing you."

Jesse tasted the wine then spat it out on the floor. Tainted. But with what? He'd noticed the seal broken when he'd pulled the cork but figured Mary June had opened it for them. He gave another taste. Peyote—almost imperceptible.

Hurrying across the room, he wrenched open the door and roared, "Mary June."

Chapter Sixteen

Only one harrowing night had passed, but Jesse exhaled his first deep breath in what seemed like days. "She's much better."

Mary June peered over his shoulder, and they both stared down at Trinity as she lay in Mary June's bed. "Yes. The worst seems to be over. She'll be fine."

Sleepy-eyed, Mary June yawned and took to a chair. They had both been up all night watching over Trinity.

"Where did you find that wine, Mary June?"

"Among Briggs's favorites, in a cubby behind the bar."

"But why would he lace it with peyote?"

"What do you mean? What's that?"

"It's made from a cactus actually. My mother studied herbs and plants, and this one especially fascinated her. It was used for centuries by the Indians living southwest of here."

"You mean like medicine?"

"Sort of, mostly for ceremonies and rituals. You can see it's extremely dangerous. Any idea why Briggs would have it around?"

A frown creased her forehead as she contemplated. "I don't know, Jesse. That's the wine he uses for his special parties. I'm so sorry. I thought it would be the best of the lot."

"You mean he's giving this to you girls?"

"No, not us. But now and then, other women show up. Then they mysteriously disappear. He uses them for big get-togethers in the backroom. That's when he brings the wine out. We've tried to talk to the women, but they aren't here long enough for us to get close to them. And around here, being nosey and asking questions results in beatings, or being fired."

Her words hit hard, but not with surprise. "I think I've seen some of the same women at the hideout. Do you know where he takes them?"

"No. Clavin hauls them off and sometimes there's men in the wagon too. And we never see them again. It happened not too long ago."

Was Briggs evil enough to be selling people as well as whiskey and good times?

Jesse headed for the door of Mary June's room. "I'd better go to work so Briggs doesn't get suspicious. If Trinity doesn't continue to improve, or she gets worse again, let me know. When she's able, get her over to my Uncle Sol's. But don't breathe a word of this to anyone else."

"All right, Jesse. Thank goodness you were able to bring her back from her hysterics. She nearly went out the window when she thought she was being chased. I don't think I could have stopped her. She listened to you. She trusted you. And by all accounts she loves you very much."

"She shouldn't."

"Who we love is not always our choice."

"Keeping them safe is."

"But Jesse—"

"Leave it alone. Don't put ideas in her head.

You've been a good friend to both of us. Maybe when all this is over, things can be different."

"All what?"

"You're better off not knowing."

He left before the expression in Mary June's eyes had him saying more. Had him saying just what she was thinking. That he did indeed love Trinity, overpoweringly so. The idea almost scared him more than getting caught by Briggs.

****

Eyes closed Trinity listened to the world around her. She remembered feeling sick—then feeling even sicker. What followed had been frightening, wonderful, hard to put into words. She'd laughed harder and more joyfully than ever before—and she'd wept, deeply, uncontrollably for her own pain and for all the ills of the world.

Colors had flashed before her eyes, and solid objects shimmered and moved about. She thought she must have gone insane. Then the voices called to her from afar, promising her she would be all right and no one would hurt her.

Mary June had been there—sweet and kind as an angel. Trinity felt as if she'd spoken to God—and this time *He* was listening. She heard birds chirping, but their voices were as loud as church bells ringing, and the nearby kerosene lamp shot rays of light around the room, spinning, spinning, spinning.

The lace on the bed jacket she wore had become a fascination. The threads dancing as if of their own volition. She watched as every stitch fell perfectly into place, and the beauty of the intricate design seemed to hold the secrets to the order of the world.

Then the fear came, and she tried to escape the prison of her mind. She stood at the window, wishing to soar higher than the clouds, feeling so insignificant compared to the scene down below. When the sun set in all its glory, she thought God must have put it in his pocket for safekeeping until morning. If she listened closely, colors made sound—sounds she could touch like gossamer webs.

And through it all, Jesse was there, a face she loved, a heart she knew. She remembered the texture of his skin, the smell of his hair, the love in his eyes.

Was it all a dream? It had felt so real. She opened her eyes. A bout of dizziness skewed her vision as she glanced around. How had she gotten here in Mary June's room?

"About time you were awake."

"Mary June, what happened?"

"The wine you drank had peyote in it. Do you know what that is?"

"No. I've never heard of it. Is it poison?"

"Not exactly. Jesse says it comes from a cactus. I guess the Indians use it for spirit ceremonies, to have visions. And after seeing you last night, I guess it really works. You were sure seeing things unbeknown to Jesse and me. You got an awfully big dose, but you should be fine. Are you hungry?"

"No, not really. But I'm more thirsty than I've ever been in my entire life."

Mary June filled a glass from the bedside water pitcher. Trinity drank it down, nonstop. Then asked for more.

"The night we planned for you and Jesse sure went all wrong."

"Oh, but Mary June, it started out so wonderful. We were talking and dancing and time seemed to stand still. I love him, I really do. So much so it scares me."

"He's afraid of the same thing."

"What do you mean?"

"Nothing. You need some food and to get back to Sol's."

"My clothes..."

"They're right here, honey. I'll help you put them on."

"How did I get to your room."

"Jesse carried you."

Trinity smiled as bits and pieces of last night came and went. She remembered being held in his arms—safe and protected.

"Where is Jesse?"

"He stayed at your side the entire night," Mary June reassured. "He only left when he knew you were coming around, saying he had work to do." She pawed through the bundle of clothing, separating Trinity's items from the ones the girls had loaned her. "That's odd," she mumbled. "There's a silk stocking gone missing."

As she dressed, Trinity thought how falling in love was changing her life and consuming her existence. But as soon as the bridge was fixed, she was supposed to leave. Yet she was no longer sure that she could.

****

Finished with tallying the accounts for Mr. Briggs, Jesse put away the books—the real set of figures as well as the forged set which funneled thousands of dollars through the saloon. The evidence against Briggs kept mounting, but he'd yet to prove who shot Jacob.

Billy Bart remained the likely suspect.

The little book he'd found yesterday had turned out to be fascinating—and horrifying. There were dates going back almost two years. Column after column listed people registered by number rather than names, followed by a basic description. Some entries included the letter P, then an amount and a notation like too much, not enough, about right, as if Briggs was trying to figure out the correct amount of peyote concoction which with to dose his victims. Besides rounding up and selling people like animals, he was experimenting on them.

The place where each person had been captured was also noted. Pueblo seemed Briggs's favorite hunting ground. Looking back, Jesse suspected Briggs housed his victims in the abandoned train depot.

When the railroad spur never made it to Prairie Ridge, the building became vacant and was up for sale for back-taxes. Jesse had scouted out the building as an investment, and he'd seen evidence of people occasionally staying there. Remnants of food and clothing—even some blood. But he'd envisioned transients down on their luck making temporary use of the building, not groups of kidnapped humans too drugged to even mount an escape.

The book, now in Sol's hands for safe keeping, was a significant piece of evidence. And time was running out. Briggs needed to be arrested and put away where he couldn't hurt anyone else. That meant Jesse coming clean on who he was and what he'd been up to.

What would Trinity think when the truth came out? And what was her true story?

Retrieving the white stocking from his pocket, he

held the bit of gossamer close. The keepsake no longer held her warmth, but the scrap of silk inspired recollections hot enough to brand his mind.

She'd never turned him in when she knew he rode with outlaws. And while he liked to think it was his sparkling personality and sexy smile that convinced her not to do so, more likely she too had something to hide. He nestled the silk stocking back in his pocket.

But why didn't she ask for his help? Pride or mistrust? Either trait was strong enough to keep her silent. He could promise her this—when she was ready to talk, he would be ready to listen.

He blew out the flame on the kerosene lantern, plunging the small closet where he worked into darkness. As he took his leave, the sound of footsteps gave him pause.

"I'm sorry last night went so wrong."

Turning he found Mary June.

"And before you ask, Trinity is much improved. And I just took her back to Sol's."

"Thank goodness and thank you for watching over her. That was quite a party you intended for the two us."

"A mutual effort on behalf of all the girls."

"Why?"

"Oh, just to say thank you for taking such good care of us."

"But how did you even know Trinity and I knew one another?"

"Mr. Briggs's girls know more about what goes on around town than most people give us credit for. We certainly know when two people ought to be together."

"I still don't understand what prompted you to

arrange such a tryst."

"Honey, you've been mooning around here for days ready to boil over. And since you evidently didn't feel you could come to one of us, willing though we all were, we figured we'd better get outside help before you exploded—or did permanent damage to yourself."

"Was it that obvious?"

"Only to a trained eye." Mary June nodded sagely.

"I see. Well, thank the ladies for their concern. But tell them in the future they are not to use their Sunday leisure time for such mischief. They should tend to their own needs, and not worry about mine."

"We will, if you will," she said over her shoulder, as she sashayed down the hall.

Jesse gave a snort of laughter. He really was quite fond of these exceptional women. And he knew Trinity was too. She had quickly gained their loyalty and friendship. Another show of independence and strength from the woman he kept thinking of as fragile and in need of protection.

He pondered why he thought her so special, but he couldn't come up with an orderly list. There were no cold, hard facts for a summation impressive enough to sway the jury of doubts ruling his logic. Maybe that, in and of itself, was the appeal.

Chapter Seventeen

The lingering effects of peyote left Trinity near exhaustion. Sol insisted she sit and read all day as he catered to her needs, and now having gone to bed early, she lay beneath the covers, her body tired, but her mind racing with thoughts.

Tree branches rustled outside the window. The muted glow of moonlight softly illuminated Jesse as he pushed aside the lace curtains and eased over the sash.

She smiled and reached out to him. Could they take up where they left off last night? Should they? Having thought things through more logically, she realized no matter how exciting, what they had intended to do was not the best of ideas.

Fully clothed, Jesse drew near, leaned over the bed, and kissed her soundly on the mouth. "Thank goodness you seem to have recovered so well." Then he sat on the edge of the bed, flexing his shoulders and neck as if they hurt.

Was he injured? Had he been fighting with the other outlaws? Filled with renewed energy she scrambled to her knees to hover at his back. "Are you all right?" Hands braced on his shoulders she leaned forward.

He captured one of her hands and kissed her fingertips. "I'm fine. Just a little stiff and sore. Briggs left orders for me to fill the coal bin at the saloon and unload the whiskey barrels."

The fear ebbed away. "But I thought he favored you."

"On occasion he still likes to remind me I'm the hired help."

Taking a chance, she massaged his broad shoulders, working the knots from his muscles. When he sighed and seemed to appreciate the effort, she continued. Was the true weight under which he struggled less physical and more like something heavy on his mind? She wanted to ask but asking meant sharing. Were they both ready for such a leap of faith?

With a murmur of contentment, he leaned sideways, raised his feet up off the floor, and stretched out on the bed. Then he drew her to his side and simply held her in his arms.

She felt no animal yearning waiting to be satisfied. No urgency or hunger to be fed. Just comfort as together they held loneliness at bay.

When she opened her mouth to speak, he placed a finger across her parted lips. "If you're willing," he said, tracing the outline of her mouth. "I'd like to do something different tonight?"

Her breath caught in her throat. She had paid strict attention to all of Mary June's instructions on pleasing a man. What could possibly have gone unmentioned? She gave a little nod of consent.

"Tonight, I just want to hold you…and talk."

The expression of uncertainty in his eyes told her this moment of truth was a big step for him as well. "Yes, please. I'd like that too."

Reaching up over his head, he fluffed the pillows cradling them. A few loose feathers spiraled into the air, drifting downward to land on his chest. He blew at the goose down. "My brother and I were notorious for pillow fights."

This glimpse of his boyhood history took her by surprise.

"We had at least one-a-week. Sometimes our high jinx earned us a spanking, but I guess we must have figured it was worth it because no matter how hard we tried not to, we always ended up in another one."

She pictured Jesse and Jacob as they had appeared in the photos. She saw them jumping on the bed, feathers and laughter filling the air. Did Jesse have any idea how lucky he was to have such memories?

"Hey. Look at that shadow on the wall." He pointed with his free hand. "It looks like a three-legged camel. Did you do that too when you were a kid? Did you see animals and monsters on your walls at night?"

She returned her gaze to his face. "My room was dark after sunset. But I didn't need light to see the monsters. They were there in my head."

He shifted and stared at her. "What do you mean?"

"They didn't give me a candle or a lantern. I worked from sunup to sundown and when it was dark, I went to sleep."

"How could your parents treat you like that?"

"They weren't my parents. They were just the people who fed me. And darkness was the least of my worries."

He stiffened at her revelations. "Is that why you ran away, Trinity?"

Was it just a lucky guess? "What do you mean?" Struggling in his arms, she tried to sit up.

"It's all right," he reassured, urging her back to his

side. "You don't owe me any explanations. I know how hard it is to trust."

She recalled the first night they had spent together at his outlaw's lair. He had held her then too, and that small comfort had kept her from being terrified beyond reason. Now, head against his chest, she heard the beating of his heart, so sure and strong, and again she felt safe in his arms. Why not tell him the truth?

"I'm an orphan, since birth, born in a foundling home. The nuns who ran the institution were out of rooms and out of funds, so they sold me to the Hatfields—local farmers. They acted out of necessity and misguided trust, but their good intentions paved the way to my personal hell.

"The Hatfields purchased me as a piece of livestock. Once grown, a valuable asset able to work the fields by day and act as servant in the house by night. They had legal right. I've seen the papers. For years, I stayed because of fear. But with help, I was finally able to leave with hope in my heart for the future. Either way it's been a lonely journey."

"Good Lord." He gave her a quick hug. "You're brave to have come so far on your own. Jacob and I lost our parents early on, but we had Sol to take care of us."

"Desperate more than brave, I assure you. What else did you and you brother do together?"

"We had one other favorite game—it was called Tickle and Torture Time in Texas."

By the time the odd phrase began to sink in, it was too late.

Jesse rippled his fingers up and down her ribs, growling as he nipped at her neck. He was merciless, and she shrieked with laughter. Finally breaking his grasp, she scrambled to her knees and fled to the other side of the bed. Jesse swatted her with a pillow. Grabbing the other sham, she hit him back, full in the face. Feigning mortal injury, he rolled on the bed, begging for mercy as he declared her the winner. Then as she dropped her guard he came at her again.

They tumbled and wrestled like puppies.

Once, he saved her from falling off the bed, strong arms rescuing her as easily as if she were a child. She clung to him and laughed so hard tears ran down her cheeks. For the first time in her life, she cried with happiness.

Breathless, they called a truce and collapsed on the mattress. She hiccupped, then sneezed. Jesse sputtered out a final spasm of laughter.

As the last of the stray feathers spiraled around them, they cuddled close again, seeking one another's warmth. A giggle escaped her. He kissed her right temple. For a moment she thought perhaps he had changed his mind about simply being together talking. But he hadn't. He pulled off his boots and arranged the counterpane over the two of them, and with a long sigh, he resumed holding her tight.

"Thank you, Trinity."

"For what?"

"Just for being you. And for helping me remember the man I used to be."

When he slipped off to sleep, she stared at him, smoothing his hair back from his brow. Tonight he had given her perhaps more than he knew. Tonight she learned the needs of the heart and soul could be as binding and worthwhile as the pleasures of the body.

Come the dawn she knew he would be gone, but

for these few hours they belonged together—if not in body, at least in spirit.

Chapter Eighteen

He'd left while Trinity still slept. They both knew he would, so instead of guilt Jesse felt only regret. Never had he spent the night just talking to a woman, sharing innocent fun, being his true self.

Recalling their pillow fight, he smiled. He did a lot of that lately, smiling at the oddest moments. It made him feel addlebrained. It also made him happy. But happiness had often played him false. He'd been happy when they moved out west. Then his parents died. He'd been happy when he graduated from college. Then his brother died. It never paid to be happy.

Curtailing his emotions, he hurried through the gambling hall and paused before Briggs's office. His rap on the door garnered no response—good. This might be his last chance to get additional evidence.

To his surprise, the office was unlocked. That meant Briggs wasn't far away. Taking a chance anyway, he stepped inside and closed the door. He needed to see what might be in Briggs' safe. Yesterday he'd observed his boss opening the strong box, his movements reflected in the solid silver humidor standing nearby. Hopefully, he could remember the sequence and numbers.

Hunkered down in front of the big chunk of metal, he gave the dial three hard spins to the right, and one turn to the left. Just like Briggs had done. Then with one ear nestled close, he eased the dial in the remembered pattern, listening as the tumblers fell into place. Fingers wrapped around the cold steel handle, he pressed down, sighing with relief as the mechanism surrendered to his touch. Another skill to add to his outlaw persona.

The contents of the vault held the marked money he'd left at the ranch hideout—still rolled up and tied with the leather thong. The bills had gone straight from Billy Bart into Briggs's hands proving a direct connection between the man and the stagecoach robberies. Two of which had resulted in the death of passengers. Jesse hadn't been with the gang on those occasions. Could he have stopped the killings? He prayed what he risked now would at least prevent someone's death in the future.

He flipped through a sheaf of legal documents, and a slow whistle escaped his lips.

Well what do you know? On top of everything else, Mr. Briggs was in the land business. Only it seemed he was buying and selling the same property multiple times, under fictitious names. Paying outrageous prices for the worthless piece of land and supposedly losing money with each sale. Another nice way to hide the money he acquired from the stage robberies.

This was credible information. But without a witness as to what he'd found, Jesse could be accused of planting the evidence. Then it would be his word against Briggs's—the man who ran the town and local authorities. He'd have to come back with a proper writ of search, served by someone higher up in Denver.

He shoved the money and documents back inside,

swung the door shut, and gained his feet.

"What's going on here?"

Turning, Jesse came face to face with Mr. Briggs, his bodyguard Clavin, and the immense bore of an old single action Army Colt.

"Nothing in particular." Despite the fact his heart had taken up residence in his throat, Jesse smiled easy and sure.

Briggs glanced around the room. "Move aside," he growled.

Stepping forward Briggs studied the safe and the position of dial. What number had it been on when he'd entered the room? Jesse couldn't remember. The man was deranged enough to keep track of something like that.

Briggs tested the handle. "Looks like he's not trying to rob me," he indicated to Clavin. "What are you really after, Mr. Smith?"

Jesse raised his hands in a show of innocence. "I came to talk to you and noticed the door was open. Thought I'd better check things out."

"I don't believe you. There's more to your actions than meets the eye."

Jesse shrugged, trying to bluff his way out of a hole so deep he could barely see daylight. "I guess time will tell."

"There's no time left." Briggs's smile gave Jesse a bad feeling. "Billy Bart warned me not trust you. And while he's no genius, his animal instincts are pretty good. Clavin saw you sniffing around the train depot, and you've been asking lots of questions around town. Whatever your game is, it's over. Time to pay the dealer."

Not quite yet, Jesse thought. There was still a hand or two to be played if he could somehow make it to Denver. He turned to take his leave.

"Where do you think you're going?" Briggs squeezed the question out around the cigar clamped in his teeth. "You're not just walking out of here free as you please."

"The parlor is full of paying customers. If you shoot me, they'll come running. And I can't promise to cooperate should you try to drag me out of here against my will."

"I don't think any of the men who frequent my establishment would dare stand against me." Briggs's smile slid from chilling to smug.

"The girls would."

They all turned toward the open doorway in which Mary June stood.

"Stay out of this, Mary June." Of all people, she should know how dangerous it was to cross Briggs. "This isn't a good time to discuss business."

She eyed the gun in Clavin's hand, but the determined set of her jaw told Jesse she wasn't going to back down. "Well," she said, "if you don't want to discuss business, how about loyalty?"

"You damn bitches better be smart enough to show allegiance to the right man," Briggs dictated. "Or you'll all be out on your collective asses, and I'll be getting me a new set of girls. They're easy enough to come by."

Mary June didn't flinch. "That's not a convincing threat anymore."

Jesse groaned.

Briggs's gaze narrowed, and a predatory

expression sharpened his features.

Realizing her mistake too late, Mary June shifted and stared at the floor.

"What is she talking about?" Briggs demanded.

Except for the ticking of the mantel clock, the room was silent as a church on a Saturday night.

Briggs nodded, sending Clavin into action. The giant of a man jabbed the muzzle of his pistol into Jesse's ribs. Jesse sucked in a quick breath and gritted his teeth.

"Start talking, Jesse. Or I'll turn Clavin loose on Mary June. He shows even less compassion toward women."

Clavin's face twisted into a salacious grin, and he grunted out something unintelligible.

Jesse's guts felt looped around his stomach. It seemed he had no choice other than to explain Mary June's ill-timed statement. "The abandoned train station went up for sale for back taxes. Some of the girls have paid off over fifty percent of what's due."

"That's impossible. They're just simple-minded females. Besides, they don't have those kinds of funds available."

"The ladies have been scrimping and saving. And those savings have netted a tidy bit of interest at the bank. I've drawn up papers for them. As a corporation they've earned at the higher rate." Jesse didn't mention he and Sol had also invested in the corporation.

"You underhanded..." Face mottled an unhealthy red, Briggs bloated up like a guinea fowl, rendering him unable to finish his sentence.

"It's all nice and legal." Jesse could feel a noose of his own making tighten around his neck.

Briggs snarled like an animal. "You like things nice and legal, do you? Then legal it shall be. I'd just as soon see you hanged as shot. We can make it an event, and I'll be relieved of responsibility." He snatched the pistol from his bodyguard. "Sit down."

Before Jesse could respond, Clavin shoved him into a chair.

Mary June gasped and made to step forward.

Briggs waved the pistol toward the door. "Clavin. Get that whore out of my sight and fetch the sheriff back here on the double."

Clavin bounded toward the door, grabbing Mary June by the arm as he began to bully her down the corridor. Jesse leapt to his feet.

"I said sit." Spittle flew from the corner of Briggs's mouth, and he slapped the barrel of the pistol across Jesse's face sending him slumping back onto the chair.

Even a man as small as Briggs held the upper hand when he stood ready to blow your brains out with a Colt forty-five.

Chapter Nineteen

Trinity stood in the deserted alleyway behind the gambling hall, the drizzly rain dampening her spirits all the more. Something was terribly wrong.

She'd tried the door at the top of the stairs, but it was locked tight. She wanted to thank Mary June and the other women for the party—disastrous as it turned out to be. Where was everybody?

Determined to find out what was going on, she slipped between the general store and the post office and made her way to the main street. As she neared the saloon from the street side, her bravado faltered. The burly man guarding the door cradled a mean looking rifle in the crook of his arm, and the disagreeable expression on his face led her to believe he was more prone to fighting than talking things out.

"Excuse me." Using the direct approach, she tried to step around him.

He roughly barred her passage with the rifle barrel. "We're closed until tonight."

"I'm not here to drink whiskey," she said frostily. "I've come to have tea with Mary June."

"She ain't receiving guests, at least not females." A smirk accompanied his reply.

Trinity felt like turning and running. Instead she stood tall and glared at him. "Why not?"

"Because Mr. Briggs said so."

"And what do you say?"

"I say whatever Mr. Briggs tells me to say."

So much for that idea.

"Now get movin'." He took a menacing step forward. "Unless you've a mind to keep me company." Rubbing his dirty thumb back and forth across the stock of the rifle, he ogled the front of her dress. "I can give you better than tea." The smell of sweat and beer hovered around him as he licked his lips and thrust his hips at her.

She backed away, then turned and ran. His laughter followed her.

Once again reaching the sanctuary of the alley, she leaned against the wall. The memory of the man's leering gaze clung to her like dirty smoke sending a shiver twisting through her. She'd felt the same way back home when her foster father or the new hired man stared at her.

At least now she knew for certain the girls were inside.

Gathering a handful of chick-pea-sized stones, she threw them at a second-floor window. The pebbles clattered against the pane of glass and scraped noisily down the side of the building.

The upstairs curtain moved, and a face appeared—Mary June.

Trinity waved frantically. Was Jesse there too? Mary June darted a gaze over her shoulder, then back to Trinity. She pointed toward the door on the upper landing, and when Trinity nodded in understanding, Mary June disappeared and the curtain swung back into place.

Trinity bounded up the steps. The door was still

locked, but a noise sounded on the other side, and Mary June's voice seeped through the barrier.

"Trinity?"

"Yes, it's me. Open the door."

"I can't."

"Why not? What's happened?"

"Mr. Briggs padlocked the door. We're locked in. He's angry with us for something we did."

"I'll get Sol and we'll come back to free you."

"No. Promise you won't do any such thing. Please. It would only make matters worse." Mary June sounded desperate.

"All right," Trinity agreed. "Do you need food or anything?"

"No. Skinny prostitutes are bad for business so at least we're being fed."

How could Jesse allow the girls to be treated so meanly? Then her stomach lurched. He wouldn't. Fear burned through her like a prairie fire. Her earlier suspicion of dread had been well founded. "Where's Jesse?"

"He's not hurt," Mary June quickly reassured, "but he's been hauled off to jail."

"Jail?" A mix of frightful images whipped through her mind, and she had to fight to concentrate on what Mary June was saying.

"I don't know all the details, but I do know Mr. Briggs. Jesse's in real bad trouble."

"But Jesse works for Mr. Briggs."

"Not anymore. Unfortunately, the sheriff still does, so watch your step around him."

Trinity stared at the door, stunned by this turn of events. Then she jumped into action and backed away from the door.

"Trinity? Trinity?" Mary June's voice grew faint as Trinity hurried down the steps.

"I'll come back as soon as I can," she hollered over her shoulder.

Outrage fueled every step she took toward the sheriff's office. Then cold reason set in, and she slowed her pace. She couldn't just burst in and demand Jesse's release. She needed a plan. As one came to mind, she rummaged in her pocket, retrieving the pencil and paper she had brought along for the girls. With a forced smile upon her lips, she marched through the door of the local jail house.

The man behind the desk glanced up, his eyes narrowing as he looked her up and down.

Her breath stalled in her chest. Behind him, tacked to the wall, a poster named her as a runaway bride. She was no such thing. She never agreed to marry anyone, especially not Harlen the hired hand. Her intended, was offering a one-hundred-dollar reward for information on her whereabouts. This was all a twisted lie. Besides, she'd turned twenty months ago. The lawyer in Denver was supposed to declare her emancipated. Then the Hatfields couldn't tell her what to do or sell her into marriage.

Were there more flyers circulating around town? Were there handbills nailed to trees and fence posts from here back to Etta's farm. She glanced again at the poster. The sketch showed a female with long flowing hair—the way hers used to be. Her pulse slowed. Thanks to Jesse, she was no longer the woman in the picture. Besides, she was here to help him no matter the consequences.

149

"Somethin' I can do for you, ma'am?"

She jumped at the sound of the sheriff's voice, her gaze snapping back to his face.

"I ain't got no time today for settling family disputes nor for shootin' rabid dogs." He sounded disappointed about the later.

"I'd like to speak with the desperado you've captured."

He raised a brow and studied her more carefully. "He ain't allowed visitors."

"But I'm not here to visit—it's my job. I'm Sol Callahan's niece and the new reporter for the Prairie Ridge Review." Had that sounded convincing? She had no idea if there even were women newspaper reporters. But then this local yahoo probably didn't know either. "What's your full name?" she asked. "I must mention you in my article."

He sat up a little straighter and puffed out his chest. "Beaufort Langford, Sheriff."

She smiled and dared to bat her eyelashes at him. Then trying to recall some of the legal jargon she'd read in the books in Jesse's room, she decided to launch her attack from another angle. "I believe section 23 of article 4 of the code of incarceration states the prisoner is to receive at least one hot meal daily provided by the sheriff at the sheriff's expense."

"Ah…well…I don't know, I never heard of no such law."

"In other words, you're telling me the prisoner is not receiving proper treatment?" She scribbled some notes on the paper she held.

"Well no. That's not what I'm saying at all."

"If you let me interview your prisoner, I will

arrange for that little oversight to be left out of my article. And I will offer in the future to provide said meal at my expense."

Leaning over the desk, she tried putting into practice the seductive techniques Mary June and the girls had taught her. This felt like her final exam, or maybe better to call it a graduation exercise.

Sheriff Langford's lips parted, and his eyes widened. "I don't know," he hedged. His gaze locked onto the bodice of her dress, his eyes now bright with a new and unsettling gleam.

She may as well ante up all her chips. "He's just a story." She nodded over her shoulder toward the jail cells. "You're the one I find really interesting. You must be the most important man in town." She had to see Jesse, touch him, feel his warmth.

The sheriff sat up straighter, sporting a self-important smile. She wanted to slap the expression from his face. Instead she smiled back, sweet as pie. "May I interview the prisoner now?"

"What about me."

"Business before pleasure." She shrugged as if the situation was not to her liking either. "The editor's waiting for my story."

"All right," he finally agreed. "You've got fifteen minutes with him, and the rest of the day with me."

Her stomach curdled at that idea. Had she played the game too well? "I can hardly wait. By the by, what time is it?"

"Only eleven o'clock," he said. "We'll have the whole afternoon to get to know one another."

"That's wonderful." She nodded. "I'm sure Mr. Briggs won't mind being kept waiting."

"Mr. Briggs?"

"Yes. I have an appointment with him in half an hour. I'm to interview him over lunch. I've never met the man, but I'm sure he'll bow to your wishes without hesitation. I'll just remind him who's in charge around here, and if he doesn't like it, he can go find another town to live in."

The sheriff blanched and leapt to his feet. "On second thought, I got paperwork that needs doin' before the circuit judge arrives for the trial. I'm too busy to be spending time with you after all."

The knot in her stomach uncurled. "Perhaps another time," she said brightly.

He stared at her as if he wasn't sure what to do next.

"The interview," she prompted.

He grunted a noncommittal response, grabbed a ring of keys off a wall peg, and stepped toward the holding cells. "Fifteen minutes," he reminded Trinity before unlocking and swinging open the iron reinforced door.

She crossed the threshold, into a shadowy realm of metal bars and cinder blocks. The door clanged shut at her back, and a rat scurried about in a dark corner up ahead. As her eyes adjusted to the dim light, she inched her way forward. Surely a castle dungeon couldn't be more cold and damp.

In the last cell, Jesse sat on the edge of a narrow bunk—his forearms on his thighs and his hands dangling between his knees. Head down and his shoulders slumped, he appeared so vulnerable—and desperately in need of a friend. Were the circumstances of his arrest so forbidding as to render him a man without hope.

"Hey, cowboy," she said, yearning to rush to his side. "You're a hard man to find."

Jesse started. The hard line of his mouth softened as he gained his feet and stepped closer to his side of the bars. She gripped the cold steel. He reached to cover her hands with his. The warmth of his touch renewed her spirit, but his words chilled her to the bone.

"Get out of here, Trinity. Right now."

"First you tell me to get out of town. Then to stop visiting the bordello. Now you don't want me here. Well guess what, mister. I'm not going anywhere. Not until you tell me what's going on. And talk fast—we only have fifteen minutes."

He tightened his grip around her hands. "I saw the poster out front with your picture on it."

His words cooled her fervor.

"You shouldn't be anywhere near a law dog, or me for that matter."

"Then where should I be?" she challenged.

"Go back to your betrothed, or whoever the guy is."

"Oh, for heaven's sake, that's a bunch of made up nonsense. No man owns me. Or at least they soon won't."

His expression softened. "You still need to get out of here. Stick with Sol. He'll know what to do."

She took note of the bluish circles under Jesse's eyes and the stubble of beard on his cheeks. His situation was desperate, his surroundings Spartan, yet he worried about her. The faith she had placed in him was elevated to an even higher level—only a good and true man would disregard his own needs to protect someone else.

"Oh, Jesse, what happened? Why are you here?"

He lowered his hands to his sides. Reaching though the bars, she rested one hand on his chest, refusing to let him push her away, refusing to run when he needed her the most.

"I've been accused of robbery—and murder."

"Murder…" The bottom fell out of her stomach. The atmosphere seemed to dim, and the blood drained from her head, leaving her lightheaded. She had refused to accept the notion Jesse was a stage robber. To believe him capable of murder seemed even more impossible.

"But you didn't—you couldn't."

His eyes turned an ebony color, and she wasn't sure she wished to understand the dark emotion reflected there. "Oh, I could." The sharp edge to his voice almost had her taking a step back. "But you're correct, I didn't."

"Then I don't understand. Who accused you of this? It was Briggs wasn't it?"

"Yes, and it's a long story. Suffice it to say he wants me silenced because I know too much about his business, and I'm not afraid to shout it from the rooftop."

"What can I do to help?"

"Nothing. Just tell Sol what's going on and stay away from here."

The determined expression in Jesse's eyes told her any argument would be useless.

He glanced toward the door to the holding cells, then returned his gaze to her face. "How did you even manage to get in here?"

"I told the sheriff I was a reporter for the Prairie Ridge Review. And don't change the subject. What can I do?"

"I told you, nothing," he repeated emphatically. "You're going to get caught in the cross-fire."

Jesse had a stubborn streak almost as big as her own—almost, but not quite. "You hardly seem in a position to protest support from any quarter."

"Just seeing you and knowing you care is enough. You look beautiful by the way."

His unexpected declaration warmed the cold fear lodged in her belly. Then she gave a little burst of laughter. "Anybody would look good in this setting,"

He glanced around. "The accommodations are a bit crude."

"I thought you outlaws were calloused and tough," she said, trying to lighten the mood, "and didn't care about creature comforts."

He gave a crooked smile and reached through the bars to stroke her cheek. "Even a polecat yearns for a warm lair and a gentle touch."

A primitive instinct to protect what she now designated as hers raged unchecked. She wanted to tear down the cold and indifferent bars separating her from Jesse. And she wanted to lose herself in Jesse's embrace. She pressed closer, slipping her arms between the bars, her hands reaching for him as the metal bruised her shoulders and hip bones. She could feel the raw energy he was forced to hold in check. How could it be these bars did not melt from the heat and wanting flowing between them?

They both jumped as the sound of a key rattled in the door down the passageway. Fifteen minutes had passed so quickly.

Jesse grasped one of her hands and kissed the palm. "Tell Sol what's happened," he ordered, "and do exactly as he says." Then he let her hand slip from his, and his expression hardened. "And don't come back here."

She knew his harsh words were his way of protecting her. But not seeing him or knowing he was all right would be a far worse fate than anything else she could imagine.

Footsteps echoed at her back.

"Whoever heard of a female reporter anyway?" Jesse mocked loudly. "You women should stay at home where you belong and leave the running of the world to us men."

"Like you men are doing such a great job. Besides, you're big news, cowboy. And we women have only begun to take our place in the thick of things. You might as well get accustomed to having me around."

Jesse balled his hands into fists, and he wore an expression of frustration—her message had gotten through loud and clear. On impulse she mouthed the words, *I love you.*

"Sheriff, get this female out of here. And in the future, I demand you keep her away from me." His voice was cold, but she hoped the fire in his eyes spoke of remembered passion, and not anger.

Sheriff Langford grabbed her elbow and escorted her non-too-gently away from the cell.

Stumbling over the main threshold she snatched her arm free and glanced back, but the heavy door clanged shut before she could capture one last cherished glimpse of the man who had become so important in her life.

"You're not going to honor his request, are you?"

Securing the lock, the man tossed the ring of keys onto the desk. "Why not? If nothing else, a man has the right to spend his last days in peace."

She couldn't let that happen. Heaven only knew what could happen to Jesse in a place like this. "But he's big news. You're big news." No response. "You're impeding the freedom of the press," she accused. "I believe that's against the law."

"Don't threaten me with the law," the sheriff warned, his eyes narrowing. "Around here I am the law."

Only one thing seemed to intimidate this man. "Mr. Briggs will be disappointed." She shook her head in dismay. "The Review promised they would circulate a daily flyer updating the townspeople on the preparations for the trial."

"Mr. Briggs?"

"Yes. He was going to personally finance the printing of the special editions. But as you pointed out, you're the law around here, and you no doubt have a perfectly good reason for kowtowing to the wishes of a no-account outlaw."

The sheriff frowned, then he scratched his head as if thinking hard made his brain itch. "On second thought, I run the damn jail, not the inmates. You can interview the prisoner ten times a day if you've a mind to. And tell Mr. Briggs he's got my full cooperation regarding the matter."

Trinity's spirits rose. Whether Jesse liked it or not, she'd be joining him tomorrow for lunch.

Chapter Twenty

The next day the rain stopped, and as if fearing to enter Jesse's dank cell, the weak noonday sunlight crept timidly over the windowsill.

Levering himself off the cot, he began another bout of restless pacing.

Like any man or animal, he wasn't partial to being caged. His chest felt tight, and it was becoming harder and harder to tolerate having his freedom usurped.

He pictured Trinity, and the churning in his stomach eased. Then his concentration slipped and her image faded, and the real world crushed in on him again. Taking a deep breath, he held on, keeping a tight rein on the jumble of emotions threatening to ride roughshod over reason.

With nothing better to do, he dragged the three-legged stool from the corner over to the high narrow window facing the back alley. Stepping up, he grabbed the bars and pulled himself to his full height as he sought a breath of fresh air. Ugh. Only a fetid back-alley smell filled his nostrils. Ignoring the stench, he worked at loosening the bar. They held fast, and even if he could somehow remove the iron work, he doubted he could squeeze through the opening to escape.

He shouldn't have dared to single-handedly take on a man like Briggs. Foolishly, he'd thought God and truth and right had been on his side. But God had apparently been busy elsewhere, and a man with no conscience cared little for what was right as his money bought his own twisted brand of truth.

And how ironic to be charged with murder, the very crime for which he sought vengeance. He should have killed Briggs when he'd had the chance—at least it would have made hanging worthwhile.

Stepping down he returned to pacing and ran one hand across his throat, and for the first time he admitted hanging was not beyond the realm of possibilities. If only there was a way to turn the circumstances to his advantage using the ideals he'd been taught and the system he championed. His best bet was assistance from the governor, but Denver suddenly seemed awfully far away.

What defense could he possibly use—or did it matter? Briggs owned the circuit judge as assuredly as he owned the local law. Otherwise he wouldn't have risked a public trial.

He had one ace in the hole, though. Briggs was unaware of all the information he'd gathered. Maybe exposing his nefarious operations at the trial would be his inside straight to freedom. A chance not only for him, but for the people of Prairie Ridge. Briggs had cheated plenty of them. With a little show of courage, these good citizens could reclaim their town as well as their self-respect. Was that asking too much?

He was tired of watching the predators of life feed upon the meek and mild, and he was tired of living a lie when all he wanted to do was to declare the truth and go on with his life. A life including Trinity.

He touched the new bruise on his right cheek. The swelling had gone down some. Last evening, Sheriff

Langford had paid him a little visit. The man was surprisingly adept with a quirt, and he had a cruel streak wider than Blue Mesa Canyon and twice as deep. Langford wouldn't catch him off guard a second time.

A key scraped in the lock, and the metal door creaked open, followed by the aroma of food. Real food, not the swill they'd served him last night for dinner and before dawn this morning.

When he glanced up, his gaze locked onto the familiar gaudy hatbox. She hadn't stayed away like he'd asked. The lonely sentimental side of him had been hoping she'd show—although he couldn't imagine why she should. He was humbled and frightened by her loyalty. He didn't deserve anything from Trinity.

The sheriff escorted her forward. "Don't give the girl any trouble." He slapped the quirt against the palm of his other hand, emphasizing his words. This time he left the door leading back to his office open.

"You don't follow orders very well," Jesse said gruffly, angling his bruised cheek away from her.

"I do if they're sensible orders."

Her stubbornness amused him. He might as well enjoy her visit because heaven help him, he wasn't strong enough to send her away again. "I'm thankful to see you, regardless."

She stood silent, as if expecting him to say more. But even if he could manage to express himself with a modicum of eloquence in these circumstances, he probably shouldn't. How could he tell her she brought softness to a world he had come to see as hard and unfeeling? How could he tell her simply caring about him had radically changed his life?

"I've brought you some decent food." Retrieving

the plate, she slid the food through the horizontal opening built into the bars for feeding prisoners. Then she set the hatbox on the chair just outside his cell. "I'll bring more tomorrow."

"You shouldn't... Thank you." Like it or not, dangerous or not, Trinity was his only link to the outside world. Sol wouldn't dare visit him. So far, being Sol's nephew hadn't come to light. If it did, the story about Jacob would come out too, and he'd lose the advantage of surprise during the trial.

Shifting, he faced her full on as he ate.

She choked back an exclamation. He must look worse than he thought.

"Merciful heaven. We have to get you out of here."

"I'm all right. Everything will work out."

"Don't lie to me, Jesse." Her piercing gaze hobbled his thoughts.

He remained silent. Lost to those eyes he'd been afraid to get to know. Blue eyes that had seen him at his worst and yet not judged him harshly. Blue eyes now ringed by dark circles of worry and uncertainty.

"I told you before, there's nothing you can do."

"That's not what Sol says."

A premonition of doom kicked at his stomach. "What do you mean?" He steeled himself for her response.

"As we speak, Sol's setting the type for a feature article on Mr. Briggs. He insists, and I quote, *The newspaper business is all about publishing the truth.*"

Jesse set the plate aside and gripped the prison bars so hard his knuckles ached. An inflammatory article, no matter how subtle, could lead to deadly consequences. "You have to stop him."

"I tried. But it seems when Sol's fighting for a cause, he won't listen to reason. And no cause is more dear to his heart than you."

More guilt swept over him. Now his uncle flirted with death on his account. "Don't let him do it."

"But why? It could help you couldn't it?"

"Yes, and it could put Sol's life in jeopardy. I won't lose him too."

"What do you mean 'too'?" she asked.

Jesse dropped down onto the bunk.

Trinity nudged the hatbox aside and took to the chair wedged up against the jail cell. He could feel the heat of her body only inches from his.

She eased her hand between the bars until her fingertips rested on his thigh. "Talk to me, Jesse. I know you're more than just a man with a gun for hire and a cynical view of life."

Her declaration slammed into him like a fist, and it felt as if an iron band constricted his heart.

"Sol told me a little bit about what happened to Jacob. And I know you lost your parents."

"Yes, and Aunt Lucinda and her child. So many people I loved."

Trinity's expression clouded. "Mr. Briggs is responsible for all that?"

"No. That evil piece of work can only take credit for Jacob's death and a few other horrible recent events."

Trinity leaned her temple against one of the bars and transfixed him with a gaze more binding than the cell itself. "Tell me."

Having little to lose, he took the chance. "Until I was twelve years old, my life was pretty uneventful, and darn near perfect. Back then we lived in Illinois. Dad worked at the John Deere factory, and Mom cleaned houses for a living. We were all so happy. Jacob was nine, and despite occasional brotherly disagreements, we shared the daily chores and the adventure of life.

"When the Colorado School of Mines opened, my father, already a self-taught geologist, decided to go to school there. Uncle Sol lived near us, and the week we were packing to move, Sol's wife, Lucinda, bore a child." He released Trinity's fingers and balled his hand into a fist. "She died giving birth and the babe soon followed. I'd never known anyone who died before. Lucinda had been gentle and full of life, and the babe was a tiny innocent."

"I found some photographs in your room," Trinity confided, "and a tintype. Is Lucinda the dark-eyed woman pictured with Sol?"

Jesse nodded and watched as sadness took its place alongside the worry in her eyes.

"The loss nearly destroyed Sol. When we moved out here, Sol came too. It was a fresh start for all of us. Jacob and I loved the wild west. We played cowboy and gunslinger, and rode around on an old mule, gray in the muzzle and gentle as a lamb. For a little while we were happy again—even Sol." Jesse tried to remember his life way back then, but the good memories were so easily obliterated by the bad.

"Then trouble arrived right on schedule. A flash flood, like the one that took out the bridge last week, tore through the canyon where dad was plying his newly earned credentials. My mother had taken him a picnic lunch for them both to enjoy. The embankment collapsed. In my mind, I pretend they died happy, in each other's arms."

Trinity bit her lower lip as if experiencing the agony he had suffered.

"When my parents died, I vowed to take care of Jacob. I promised we'd always be together."

He nearly choked on the words. Like bitter poison foul and festering, ridding himself of the venomous memories felt good, but the curative was also excruciating.

"Knowing his work might be dangerous, Father took out a life insurance policy. Sol had banked the money and it gained interest. By the time I grew up there was enough money to almost pay all my tuition to Harvard University. The plan was for me to get an education, then come back to help Jacob to follow his dreams. I went to Boston and buried myself in my studies. Money was tight, but I didn't care. I lived on day-old bread and handouts from the owner of the tavern where I worked part-time. During my absence Sol and Jacob moved from Golden, Colorado to Prairie Ridge. And Sol set up his newspaper office. Then a few years ago, Mr. Briggs moved to Prairie Ridge too.

"While I was away, Jacob was killed—my kid brother, my best friend. I wasn't there when he needed me. I wasn't even there to say goodbye."

His words pummeled their way out of the dark hole where they always hid. And the only opiate alleviating his suffering came in the form of the vengeance he sought.

"Why did they kill him?" Her voice was gentle, barely more than a whisper.

He exhaled long and deep. "Jacob had evidence of

a murder arranged by Briggs. He wouldn't be bought off, and with more than enough guts to go to the authorities with the information, Jacob's honor sealed his fate. He never had a chance."

"You've endured so much, lost so many people you loved."

God above, what if he lost her too. "Find someone else, Trinity."

"I don't understand."

Of course, she understood. He hadn't missed her silent I love you yesterday. But he was nothing but trouble—a disillusioned man. He didn't believe in the law anymore, neither God's nor Man's. But the way Trinity was looking at him right now, he almost believed in himself.

"Never mind," he said softly. He couldn't leave her with no hope.

"You're right. There'll be other times for us," he lied.

"Tell me how it will be. Tell me what we'll do together."

He sought words from the books and poems he'd read, conjuring a world he wished they could share. "We'll make love in the sun, naked and warm. Then as night weaves its enchantment we'll make love again with a million stars all around. And our hopes and dreams will be as boundless as the sky."

"And with the coming of the dawn?"

"Then we'll stare into one another's eyes and wonder how we could still be alive after such passion. And by the light of day, we'll hold one another tight, never to be separated again."

"Yes." She sagged against the bars. "We'll be

together, always."

Then the tough, practical side of her took over. "But that can't happen until we prove your innocence. What you need is a good lawyer."

"I am a good lawyer. I'm just not a terribly good outlaw."

****

Standing in the parlor at Sol's house, staring at nothing in particular, Trinity prayed Jesse's romantic words were not born of desperation. She wanted to believe him with all her heart, but trust was still a new commodity in her inventory of emotions.

After reading the books in his room, she'd already guessed he'd been formally educated. That's how he knew about Shakespeare and accounting and investments. But thanks to Sheriff Langford's uncanny knack for untimely interruptions, she hadn't learned many details about his becoming a lawyer.

"How's Jesse?"

"Merciful Heaven, Sol. You near gave me a heart seizure."

"I'm sorry," he said. "I thought you heard me come in."

"He's being stoic, but it looked like the sheriff hit him, and the conditions aren't good. He told me he's a lawyer. And about what happened to Jacob."

"Jesse took a big risk confiding in you." Sol headed toward the front of the house and print shop. "No one else in these parts knows about his occupation, or that he's my nephew and Jacob's brother."

"I won't tell anyone."

"I figured we could count on you. I just wanted to be sure you understood the situation. Now we'd best get started on the evening special edition."

Jesse's warning echoed in the back of her mind. "What exactly are you going to print?"

Sol donned his ink-stained apron and rolled up his sleeves. "Nothing that might tip Jesse's hand, but we have to light a fire under the people of this town."

That didn't sound reassuring.

"We're going to plant a few seeds of truth in the fertile but misguided minds of the public."

"Jesse wouldn't want you putting yourself in danger."

Sol just smiled. "Jesse isn't here."

She helped him drag a stack of paper toward the printing press.

"If the people of Prairie Ridge would listen to their consciences rather than the voices in their nightmares, we could take back this town and live like full grown men and women instead of frightened children. The judge wouldn't dare go against the lot of us, and for once the jury could base their decision on fact, not fear."

"I think you're expecting an awful lot, and it's sure to rile up Mr. Briggs."

Sol squared his stooped shoulders as best he could, and his expression hardened. "I'm willing to take the chance if you are."

"What do you want me to do?"

Sol patted her cheek. "Just pray it's not too little, too late."

Her heart skipped a beat. "Why would you think that?"

"Because they're already building a scaffold for the hanging."

Chapter Twenty-One

The loudest noise she'd ever heard catapulted Trinity to wakefulness.

What was happening? A twister, an earthquake?

She slid from the bed and peered through the darkness. The wood floor felt oddly warm on her bare feet, yet stark apprehension chilled her to the bone. Why was it so hard to breathe?

Stumbling to the window, she threw open the drapes. The dull light of another rainy dawn seeped in through the window betraying the presence of wispy smoke curling along the floorboards.

Fire. The house was on fire!

She ran across the room, flung open the door, and rushed into the hall. "Sol," she screamed and stopped short. A charred hole occupied the space where the steps once stood. Smoke rushed up through the opening, burning her eyes and parching her raw throat. Grabbing a fold of her nightdress, she pressed the fabric to her nose and mouth to filter out the poisonous air.

Edging forward, she leaned over the gutted stairwell. Except for the random pop of a hot timber, the house was deathly still. "Sol, where are you?"

"Miss Trinity?" His voice sounded thick and muffled as it clawed its way up through the smoke-filled opening. "Are you all right up there?"

"Yes," she croaked, her throat already hurting from

169

breathing in the foul air. "But I'm trapped."

"The fire is out, but the stairs are no good. Go back to your room. Then climb out the window and down the tree. I'll be waiting at the bottom."

"Yes, all right. I'm on my way."

Smoke swirled around her ankles and trailed in her wake as she followed Sol's instructions. Raising the window, she gathered her nightdress and prepared to climb over the sash. Then she hesitated and ran to the bureau. Wrenching open the draw, she grabbed the little wooden box and tintype. Wrapping them in the dresses once belonging to Lucinda, she dropped the bundle out the window.

Easing her legs out over the sill, she braced herself and leaped into the waiting arms of the big oak. As she flailed toward a limb to get a better hold, pointy twigs cut into her thigh and scraped along her ribs.

"Don't look down."

Sol's warning came too late.

In the hazy light of daybreak, the ground below appeared a country mile away. Eyes shut tight, she clung to the bough like a treed possum. Falling and breaking her neck seemed a terribly silly way to die.

Her mind went blank. Then visions of another tree and another time replaced the panic. Years ago— young, fearless, and driven by hunger—she'd trespassed onto the neighboring property and climbed a big apple tree. That's when a voice had called out from below, changing her life forever. That's when she'd met Etta.

"What you doin' up there, girl?" She'd been caught by the gray-haired woman who lived all alone with a blue-ticked hound and a big black cat. The townspeople called Etta Matthews a witch, and crazy to boot. Trinity thought she might die on that day too. Instead, she had truly begun to live. Her death-grip slackened. Neither crazy nor a witch, Etta had also taught her to face her fears.

"You might commence moving a bit faster," Sol encouraged. "I was on the ground floor when the explosion went off, and I was able to stop the fire from spreading. But it had a pretty good foothold on the front of the house and could have rekindled."

Etta's image faded to a warm memory, and angry at being a fraidy-cat, Trinity opened her eyes and rallied her nerve. Half scrambling and half falling, she reached the ground, reeling to one side. Sol grabbed her arm and kept her upright.

"You all in one piece?" he asked, looking her over.

"I...I think so."

"Not being able to get up the stairs to you gave me a terrible fright." Concern knitted his brow, but gentleness guided his gnarled old hands as he brushed the leaves and twigs from her clothes and hair.

Feeling like a six-year-old with a loving parent, she momentarily reveled in Sol's attention. "I'm fine, really."

Reassured, he turned to stare at the house. "I suppose we'd best go check for those hot spots and see what we can salvage. Maybe find a ladder to put up in place of the stairs."

"Wait." Retrieving the bundle of dresses from the ground, she unwrapped the box and photo, placing them into Sol's hands. "At least you needn't worry about these being lost to fire or ruined by the smoke."

He shook his head and clutched the mementoes to

his chest. "I especially cherish the one of Lucinda." Tears welled in his eyes. "Our memories are what matter most in the long run. Thank you for saving mine."

They turned toward the house in unison, and a great peal of thunder split the quiet as rain pelted down. On the run, they reached the backdoor and scrambled inside. Sol set the box of photos on the kitchen counter. Waves of heat surrounded them as they picked their way over the rubble and boards once belonging to a stairway. They found no live flames, but the worse damage lay ahead in the print shop, where the heart of the explosion had occurred.

As they entered the room, Trinity gasped at the devastation.

The printing press, now a twisted hunk of metal and rubber, lay forlornly on its side, and hundreds of little block-letters were strewn around the room like the petals of wildflowers after a storm. Sol's ink-stained leather apron lay smoldering in a corner. The front window was blown out—gusts of wind periodically sending sheets of rain through the opening.

Using the toe of his boot, Sol prodded the printing press as if it were a sick animal he could encourage back onto its feet. The bleak gesture carved a hollow space even sadness couldn't fill.

"Damn hooligans." He stepped to the center of the room and glanced around at the carnage. "Briggs has some nasty boys on the payroll willing to follow his orders no matter what."

"This is what Jesse was worried about—retaliation for last night's special edition."

Sol turned to face her. "He was correct, and the

lines are drawn. It's a real war now."

"Will they come back to the house?"

"Most likely. But we won't be here."

She stiffened. "What do you mean? We can't turn tail and run. Not when Jesse still needs our help."

Ignoring the question, Sol stepped to the roll top desk which had survived the blast with minimal damage. "Ever shoot a gun before?" He unearthed a pistol from the depths of the drawer on the right.

A gun... She wasn't partial to firearms—they were for killing things. "I shot a rifle on the farm. It was a terrible experience."

Sol straightened and turned to face her. "What happened?"

"Pa Hatfield told me I had to kill the fox worrying the hen house. I refused, pointing out it made more sense to put up a better fence, but he was a lazy brute. He whipped me every time another hen turned up dead. After a few weeks, I gave in. I fired two shots, missed the fox, wounded a chicken, and put a hole in Mother Hatfield's favorite milking pail. I got whipped again that night, but the fox got away."

Sol's eyes turned cold. "I'm sorry for what happened to you. I don't abide violence, especially when it comes to women and children. On the other hand, I'm getting too old to passively wait around for some events to take their natural course. It's your decision whether or not you use this." He held up the pistol. "I just want you to have the option."

When he put it like that, she felt less threatened. Yet to have at your command the power to so quickly and easily end another person's life was a great responsibility.

"Don't worry about your aim," he continued. "It'll improve noticeably when your life depends on it. Besides, pistols are for close range. You won't miss." He gathered up a handful of bullets. "This is a single action Army Colt with a cartridge conversion. You must cock the hammer back before you fire. The cylinder holds six rounds, but I suggest you carry only five keeping the hammer on the empty chamber unless in use."

He loaded the cylinders, handling the gun as comfortably as if it were a coffee grinder or a candle mold. She doubted she would ever be so relaxed around a revolver.

"It's people that kill, not guns. Just don't point it at anything unless you're committed to pulling the trigger and taking the consequences."

Too dry-mouthed to speak, she nodded in understanding.

"When you do fire," he continued, "expect a lot of noise, and you won't be disappointed. And mind you hold the gun with both hands. Despite its weight, the .45 caliber kicks like a mule on red-eyed whiskey. But it shoots true, and if nothing else it's big enough to scare any man with half a brain if he's looking down the barrel."

"Why are you teaching me all this?"

Sol glanced around the room, and his expression hardened. "We can't stay here. I want you to let a room at the hotel, and I need to know you can take care of yourself. Once you're settled in, you're to lay low and stay put." A gruffness she'd never heard before edged his voice. "Take your meals in your room and don't go near Jesse or the jail. Do you understand?"

"Yes. But…"

"No buts about it, Miss Trinity. You swear to do as I say, or I'll take you with me—and it promises to be a rough trip."

A new terror squeezed at her heart. "Where are you going?"

"I'm going to try to get to Denver. If I'm lucky, two days out, and two days back. No stopping, except for necessity."

"Denver? But with all the rain, the river between Prairie Ridge and Denver is still running high."

He nodded. "Then I better find a horse that can swim. The dynamite was more than just a means of putting us out of business. It was a warning to all the good citizens of Prairie Ridge. And unless I miss my guess, the noise sent even the most stouthearted folks scurrying back to their rabbit holes. Jesse won't get any support from the townspeople now—or a fair trial. All he's got is us, and we're going to need help."

Sol pressed the loaded revolver into her hands.

The firearm felt nearly as heavy as the dread filling her heart.

****

Jesse couldn't obliterate the horrible sound from his mind.

Near dawn he'd heard a powerful explosion, the blast coming from the direction of Sol's house. It sounded like the end of everything he held dear. If he didn't stop thinking about what might have happened, he'd go mad at the imagining.

The door of the holding area swung open. Sheriff Langford entered, strode forward, and slammed down a bucket of fresh water in front of his cell.

Jesse thrust his arms out between the bars, making a grab for the man's shirt. "What the blazes was all that noise about?"

Langford sidestepped out of reach. His mouth twisted into a taunting grin. "That's for me to know and you to find out. But I'll tell you one thing for sure. I wouldn't expect no visit today from that reporter gal of yours."

The sheriff's words left Jesse all the more worried. Had his worst fears been realized? He'd told her not to get involved, to stay away. And then like a fool, he'd been glad when she came back. And what about Sol?

"You cold hearted…. Tell me what's going on."

The sheriff's derisive smile turned into a full-out sneer. "I don't have to tell you nothin'. Besides, what you gonna' do about it? Cooling your heels in a jail cell, you're as useless as a gelding on a stud farm."

The sheriff was correct, and Jesse realized he was almost angrier with himself than at the pitiful excuse of a man standing before him.

After months of planning, how had it come down to this? He'd become impatient. And in his haste for this to all be over, he'd been careless and made mistakes. Why? Because he'd met Trinity and fallen in love with her, and after that nothing else had seemed to matter.

She had to be alive. The thought of losing Trinity became a physical agony, turning his blood to ice, and the pain ripped through him hard and deep until he wanted to howl like a wounded animal. God, please let her be safe. He'd rather die a tortured death than live one moment without her. He swallowed hard and forced himself to speak.

"Why should I care what happens to that woman? Her and that rag of a newspaper mean nothing to me." Afraid his face would betray his true feelings, he turned away and lounged against the wall.

"Nice try," the sheriff countered. "You must be in cahoots with her and the old man that runs the operation."

Jesse's spirits rose. Langford hadn't referred to Trinity or Sol in the past tense. If they were dead Langford wouldn't pass up the opportunity to brag and gloat and twist the knife. "How do you figure I have anything to do with them?"

"Because the Prairie Ridge Review has changed from printing local gossip to local politics, and you're headline news."

He stifled a groan. Sol had gone ahead and printed an inflammatory article. The man was a master of understatement, loving nothing better than to parry words.

"Mr. Briggs wasn't too impressed with the new format. In fact, he took particular exception to some of the material."

"And," Jesse prompted.

"And the explosion you heard was Mr. Briggs cancelling his subscription. His and everybody else's." Langford emitted a hoot of laughter and sauntered away. "The old man won't be printing any special editions tonight."

Jesse clenched his jaw and held his silence as another loop of concern was added to the knot already twisted around his guts. At least he knew they were alive.

The main door clanged shut, and the scream of

total solitude reverberated through his brain. Maybe now Trinity would understand why she had to keep her distance. In anger, he grabbed up the three-legged stool and smashed it against the stone wall. It shattered, and his mind felt ready to do the same.

He needed to see her and touch her—just for a moment.

****

It continued to rain all day and into the night. Then the wind came up blowing the clouds away, revealing a butterball of a full moon hovering low in the sky.

Trying to keep to the shadows, Trinity made her way down the boardwalk from the hotel to the jail. Guilt at disobeying Sol dogged her steps. Then she thought of Jesse alone and abandoned, and nothing else mattered.

Surely Jesse had heard the explosion. She had to let him know she and Sol had survived, and Sol was on his way to Denver. She had to let him know they hadn't deserted him in his fight for his innocence.

She glanced around, her nerves on edge. Everything appeared different in the dark. Still afraid to handle the big gun, she'd left it hidden beneath the mattress at the hotel. Too late, she realized she was even more afraid to be without the weapon.

As she scurried past the saloon, the swinging doors burst open and two men pitched out onto the walkway. Swearing loudly, they flailed punches at one another and tumbled into the muddy street. A raucous crowd, whooping and hollering, funneled out the door in their wake. Hoping everyone's' attention was focused on the brawl, Trinity drew her shawl closer and hurried on into the night.

As the riotous sounds dwindled to a dull roar, she reached a towering platform and stopped. Hiding amongst the wooden struts, the scent of fresh-cut pine filled her nostrils. The structure must be new. Glancing up, she stifled a scream. This was the scaffold for Jesse's hanging.

Her stomach heaved and she stumbled, trying to get away from the symbol of death. Then she rushed down the alley leading to the backside of the jail.

The window of Jesse's cell seemed much higher from the outside. Even on tiptoe she couldn't quite reach the bars. "Jesse," she whispered. No answer. Did she dare risk speaking any louder? Poking around in the mud with the toe of her boot, she searched for something to throw.

****

A rock sailed through the barred window, ricocheting off his cell wall with the horrifying clang of a church bell.

Jesse lurched to his feet. Before he could reach the window, another stone whizzed past his head and skidded out into the corridor. What the heck? Whoever was in the alley was making enough noise to be heard in Denver.

Having smashed the stool, Jesse dragged his bunk over to the wall, the wooden legs bumping along the uneven floor. Climbing onto the unsteady cot he grabbed the bars and peered out into the night.

A cat screeched, and a female voice shooed it away—Trinity.

"What are you doing here?"

"I had to see you."

"Are you all right?"

"I'm fine, and so is Sol."

What a relief. Then he stiffened as a noise sounded at his back.

"What the hell is goin' on in here?" The sheriff burst though the outer door.

Jesse nearly jumped out of his skin as he leaped down from the cot.

"Who's in the alley?" the sheriff demanded.

"Don't get riled—it's just a cat."

"Cat my ass," Langford snarled. He glared at Jesse then hurried away, no doubt going to investigate for himself.

Jesse bounded back onto the cot and reached through the window toward Trinity, the edge of the cinder blocks cutting into his arm.

"Trinity, you've been found out. The sheriff's coming." Their fingers touched—a moment of warmth, a moment of hope. Then his fear for her won out.

"Run, dammit."

Her fingertips brushed across his palm. Then she was gone, lost to the darkness, and his world again turned cold and bleak.

Chapter Twenty-Two

Trinity glanced out the hotel window. The sun continued to turn its back on what was happening in Prairie Ridge. Her mood seemed just as dark.

Jesse was no longer allowed visitors. And newly sworn-in deputies stood guard in the back alley preventing any repetition of her late-night escapade. The forced separation added to her worry for both Jesse and Sol.

From the second floor, she observed Sol's boarded up newspaper office and also the dilapidated church that would be used as a courthouse during the trial.

According to Mary June, religion had survived only briefly in Prairie Ridge. Belief in a higher power made people strong, giving them a reason to unite and the will to fight. Wanting the souls of the people as well as their money and allegiance, Mr. Briggs had driven off every preacher who tried to bring the word of God to town.

Would God show pity today for the town that had forsaken Him?

Shifting her gaze to the left, she could barely make out the corner of the jail house. Two days had passed, and Jesse's trial was scheduled to begin shortly.

The circuit judge, located up in Greeley, had been able to travel south to Prairie Ridge along the backroads and between the swollen rivers. He arrived yesterday.

By all accounts, he'd looked formidable. The jury had been commandeered shortly thereafter. They looked intimidated.

Trinity feared being a lawyer wasn't going to get Jesse out of this one. Life here was governed by power, not fairness—the same rules her guardians used. And while she hadn't been able to fight back physically while growing up, she had protected her thoughts and dreams. Jesse must do the same and not lose sight of who he was and what he fought for.

She rubbed her fingertips across the uneven scar on her left forearm. The Hatfields had broken her bones on occasion, but they had never broken her spirit. And no one was going to break Jesse's. She'd be there for him in the courtroom. Let him know he wasn't alone.

Jesse needed her as no one in her life ever had. Etta had loved, protected, and educated her. But Etta could and would survive without Trinity. This was different— and she needed Jesse as much as she believed he needed her. These were compelling emotions, and dangerous. They made her vulnerable, and vulnerability went against the rules of survival.

A floorboard creaked in the hallway. She spun around and lunged for the revolver she now kept on the dresser. The muffled sounds became definite footsteps.

Barely breathing, she cocked back the hammer and aimed dead center at the door.

After a heart-stopping pause, the person moved on.

She slumped in relief and eased the hammer back down, then rotated the cylinder around to the empty chamber.

Day or night, the scurrilous hotel was a symphony of uneasy sounds. Some noises raucous and abrupt, others unnerving in their furtiveness. All were unwelcome.

She was thankful now Sol had insisted she take the revolver. The weight alone was a comfort, the stark beauty oddly compelling. She'd slept with it beneath her pillow instead of under the mattress.

Shoving the bulky revolver into her purse, along with extra cartridges, she headed out.

On her way to the church, she made a detour to the bordello. Still reduced to speaking to her friends through the locked door, she pegged a rock at Mary June's window, and then hurried up the back stairs to wait for her.

Hands braced against the wood, she could feel the dampness oozing out of the cracks and knotty holes. A faint rustle of silk announced Mary June's arrival on the other side of the barrier.

"Hi, darlin'. You on your way to the trial?"

"Yes."

Apparently, Mary June kept well informed. Between sweet-nothings the customers no doubt whispered rumors about Jesse's imprisonment and the upcoming trial.

"How are you and the girls faring?"

"We're doing fine. Don't be frettin' over us. And we've been practicing our reading and writing every day," Mary June added proudly. "Before long we'll be the most literary ladies of the evening west of the Mississippi and north of the Pecos."

Trinity couldn't help but smile. "You should start charging more for your services."

"A valid point. I'll bring it up for discussion at dinner tonight. Of course, most of our customers don't come here to be read to." The happiness in her voice withered as her words turned serious. "What's the real lowdown on Jesse?"

Trinity laid her cheek against the rough wood, fighting back a sob. "I'm scared, Mary June. After the explosion at the newspaper office, no one in town will come to his defense. I don't think he has a chance."

"What does Sol say?"

"He's gone to Denver to ask Governor Adams for help. But he hasn't returned."

"What's taking so long?"

"With the river still overflowing, I don't know if he's even gotten there yet. What can I do for Jesse on my own? They won't even let me see him."

"You're not alone, Trinity. If you need help, the girls and I will find some way to bust out of here. We'll be there for you and Jesse."

"Thank you. I believe you would. And I might become desperate enough to ask."

****

Rain spit down from a sullen sky as Trinity joined the crowd heading for the church, but the weather turned out to be the least of her worries. Sheriff Langford prowled around the front entrance, confiscating weapons from the men attending the trial and actually refusing entrance to certain people— apparently at his discretion.

She hung back, then noticed the approach of a large woman wearing a fluttering cape and a big, floppy-brimmed hat. Crouching down and concealing herself on the far side of the formidable lady, Trinity slipped past Langford during the flurry of activity.

All the seats were already filled. Pushing and

shoving her way forward along the wall, Trinity positioned herself near a pillar with a clear view of the newly erected judge's bench. She'd gotten there just in time.

A murmur rumbled through the room with the subtlety of an avalanche, and with heads down, the jury shuffled in and took their seats. Then the sheriff stepped forward, setting events into motion.

"All rise. Court is now in session. The honorable Reginald T. Pettibone presiding."

The assemblage rose. Trinity didn't like the looks of the judge. With his hair fancy-trimmed and slicked back with pomade, he swept grandly into the room as if entering an opera house rather than a court of law. And with every step he took, his boots flashed from beneath his long black robe. They were shiny and expensive looking.

The pinkish softness of his face and hands indicated if he'd ever known manual labor it wasn't recently. Mounting the raised platform with pomp and ceremony, he cast disparaging looks down from his bench.

"You may be seated." A sigh accompanied the statement, as if it were a chore to inform them.

Her last thread of hope for a fair trial snapped when the judge narrowed his eyes and glared at the jury. No words seemed necessary. To a man, each juror cringed like a whipped hound. Trinity recognized pee-in-your-pants fear and blind obedience. Only a miracle would win over these poor sodbusters and shopkeepers. No doubt they favored the preservation of their own lives over Jesse's.

All of a sudden, the main doors to the church

rattled and swung inward. Expectation hung in the air, smothering every sound until only tomb-like silence remained. Jesse stood motionless in the open portal wearing jeans and the black shirt she'd brought him previously. Eyes ablaze with righteous fury, he seemed a dark avenger come to do battle with words and logic. He might fare better with a sword or gun.

Two brawny guards prodded Jesse forward. Metal handcuffs and leg chains gleamed on his wrists and ankles. A lesser man might have wavered under the mental strain and physical weight, but not Jesse. He walked at his own pace, refusing to be hurried along. A stubble of beard shadowed his face and honed the determined angle of his jaw. The man she loved had never appeared more handsome, or more dangerous— or more deeply mired in trouble.

****

Where was she? Knowing Trinity would never stay away, Jesse had lived for the moment of seeing her again. Slowing his pace, he searched for her in the sea of faces.

One of the deputies stiff-armed him from behind, and he nearly tripped on the heavy chain dragging between his feet. They herded him along like a beast, and he felt like gnashing his teeth. Instead, he forced his expression to stony indifference and proceeded down the aisle.

The jury members were all strangers. But up ahead was a familiar face. Billy Bart. He sat beside Mr. Briggs—ready to fetch, roll over, or kill on command. The small-brained, but hugely effective Clavin was also nearby. Knowing Sol was in transit between here and Denver, he didn't bother to search for his uncle.

At the altar of the church, Jesse halted and wrenched free of the guard on his left.

"If you please, gentlemen." Judge Pettibone waved the two men aside. "You have my permission to shoot the defendant should he try to escape. There's no need to hover over him."

The judge had a way with words.

Peering down from above, the man cleared his throat as if it were a prelude to greatness. "It is my understanding that you have waived your right to proper counsel. And you are suffering under the delusion that you can defend yourself."

Jesse's indignation rose a notch. "Considering my circumstances, it seemed prudent to retain the most competent man in town."

"And what gives you the audacity to think you could possibly be suited for any form of livelihood other than robbing stages and murdering people in cold blood?"

"A diploma from Harvard law school."

A collective gasp rose from the spectators, and the jury leaned forward.

The judge raised his brows in surprise but quickly recovered. "Even if what you say is true, Mr. Smith, I'm told a man who speaks in his own defense has a fool for a lawyer."

Jesse shrugged. "With all due respect, your Honor, it's doubtful one fool more or less will be noticed in this judicial circus."

Guffaws rippled through the crowd, and even the jury emitted a sound resembling laughter. The judge turned an unhealthy shade of purple. Then he slammed his gavel down hard enough to drive a railroad spike through seasoned mahogany. "Order in the court. Order in the court. Another such outburst and I'll have the room cleared. And as for you, Mr. Smith, I'm extremely close to holding you in contempt of court."

Was that supposed to strike terror in his heart?

"It would be a refreshing change from being falsely accused of murder." He strode toward the defense table with as much dignity as his shackles would allow.

This time the murmur reverberating through the room was more subdued. Yet not tolerating any show of rebellion, the judge again bludgeoned the top of his bench bringing the crowd to a discontented silence.

Jesse risked another glance at those gathered to watch the show. There she was—half-hidden behind a wooden column. In his mind, Trinity sparkled like a wallflower in morning sunlight. He couldn't suppress the tiniest of smiles.

Trinity's expression remained controlled—her lips barely curving in reply. What he wouldn't give to feel the warm embrace he knew she would offer without question or hesitation.

She raised her hands, and then clenched them together against her chest as she stepped back, pressing up against the wainscoting as if she too fought against the urge to rush forward, to hold and be held.

He mustn't draw attention to her. He stood a bit taller and turned away. As her image slipped from his field of view, a ragged breath tore at the back of his throat, and Judge Pettibone's voice cleaved through his preoccupation.

"Let the record show formal charges shall now be read. The sheriff having the right to offer further details and to call witnesses as he sees fit to corroborate the facts."

More likely to collaborate their fictitious story. Still, Jesse listened carefully. They had yet to tell him who he was accused of killing. That little omission had made preparing a defense rather difficult.

"The accused, Jesse Smith, is charged with three counts of armed robbery, the dates listed herein, and two counts of first-degree premeditated murder. According to witnesses, on the thirtieth day of May, in the year1888 the defendant did forcibly abduct a young woman from the Whitaker Stagecoach line. He then took her to his hideout, and after using her for unspeakable acts, he did kill her the next day by means of slitting her throat."

The room was so silent Jesse could hear truth and sanity dying by the inch.

"Said victim," the sheriff continued, "is described as a young female, small of stature, with blue eyes and long blonde hair."

Jesse was stunned.

As if stricken by some hideous madness, he fought down the urge to roar with laughter. He was being accused of killing Trinity. Of killing the one woman he would die for, the one woman whom he felt he would die without.

A shuffling noise sounded at his back, and his surprise turned to dread.

He glanced over his shoulder. No no no...

Trinity had abandoned the refuge of the shadows. She was going to turn herself in to prove his innocence. He couldn't let this happen. Had to stop her.

Face too pale and eyes too wide, she opened her mouth to speak.

Chapter Twenty-Three

"Stop. I object," Jesse aimed the words at the judge, but he meant them for Trinity. Arms raised, he jangled his manacles and strode forward with a flourish, drawing all attention in his direction.

"What is it now, Mr. Smith?" The judge's words were edged with warning.

From the corner of his eye Jesse saw Trinity draw back into the shadows, and the tightness in his chest uncoiled. He admired Trinity's courage but coming forth would be a pointless sacrifice putting her in danger and doing him no good.

"I demand to know the name of the alleged murder victim."

"We aren't sure who she is, or was," the sheriff admitted. "Only that she's dead and you killed her."

What a dull-witted oaf. Day after day Langford sat at his desk with his nose two feet away from Trinity's missing person poster, yet he hadn't associated the description of the murder victim with the description of the runaway woman. Nor had he recognized Trinity when she stood before him.

"And the body?" Jesse pressed on. "Where is it?"

"We don't rightly know that either. But we have reason to believe the murder took place near Blue Mesa Canyon."

Briggs's arrogance was amazing. The man was so

sure of himself he was betting everything on trumped up charges a first-year law student could refute. Of course, when you owned the judge and jury, maybe little things like evidence and motive were incidental.

"Do you have an eyewitness to the crime?" he demanded.

"Sort of."

"Sort of you have a witness, or you have a witness who sort of saw the crime?"

"Enough." The Judge threw the word down like a gauntlet. "This is no time for cross examination. We are merely here for the reading of the charges."

"And I am merely questioning the validity of those charges."

Billy Bart jumped up and faced the jury. "I saw the knife Jesse used," he crowed. "It was covered in blood."

"Coyote's blood is as red as a man's or a woman's," Jesse pointed out.

"Meaning what?" Sheriff Langford growled.

"Meaning your evidence is circumstantial. Your best witness is a known criminal, and no matter how you sing and dance you have no corpus delicti. I recommend all charges be dropped immediately."

The room exploded with speculation.

Judge Pettibone clenched his jaw. "Motion denied. And settle down, dammit. This court will come to order."

"Who is the second person I allegedly murdered."

"The killing took place October 21st, 1887."

Jesse gripped the table, girding himself for the Judge's next words.

"This time we have a name—it's Jacob Callahan."

"What'a ya say to that, Mr. Fancy lawyer," the sheriff gloated.

"I say you just accused me of killing my little brother."

The room boiled over with noise and confusion, and no amount of gavel pounding or yelling on the part of Judge Pettibone had any effect on the chaos. He finally aimed a look of malice at Mr. Briggs, and bellowed, "Court dismissed."

****

Trying to reach Jesse, Trinity fought her way upstream against the wave of people being driven from the church at gunpoint. A losing battle, she gave up and surrendered to the onslaught, allowing the current of humanity to sweep her back out the door and down the steps.

Astounded by the turn of events, she drifted aimlessly along Main Street. Poor Jesse. How awful to be accused of killing his own brother—and her. Would it help Jesse's case if they knew she was alive? Should she go back and tell the truth and take the consequences? But with Sol still away, if they locked her up, Jesse would have no one on the outside to help him.

Stay or go—either choice left her heartsick. She didn't know what to do. But Trinity knew without a doubt he'd rather protect her at the risk of his own safety—like he'd done since they'd first met.

Jesse had fought valiantly today, daringly. Bandit or barrister, he played the part with honor and passion. She thought he must love the law. She'd noticed the confident expression on his face as he took command of the room. His eyes had glowed almost as brightly as when he'd looked at her.

****

Grabbing Jesse by the arm, the sheriff hustled him toward a side door of the church. Regardless of who had won the first battle, gut instinct told Jesse the war with Briggs had just begun.

"Wait," the judge called out. "I'd like a word with the defendant before you return him to his cell." Was there curiosity in the Judge Pettibone's voice as well as anger? "I'll summon you when I'm through, sheriff."

Langford appeared confused, then grunting in understanding, he wandered off to a discreet distance and played with his revolver.

Clavin glowered in a nearby corner.

"The charges against you are serious," the judge began, "and should you be found guilty, the punishment will be extreme."

Jesse gave a snort of laughter. "Does it make your hands less bloody when you use a euphemism for hanged by the neck until dead?"

"My hands are not the issue here." As if guilt did plague him, the judge slipped his inside the black robe he wore.

"They will be."

"Is that a threat?"

"No. It's a fact. You remember facts, Judge Pettibone. Cold, hard facts. Those important yet elusive truism which we both swore to evaluate and weigh in the pursuit of justice."

Something akin to regret shadowed the judge's expression. A muscle in his cheek twitched, and he suddenly seemed older. Did he remember what it had been like before he crossed the line, before he had betrayed his principles and integrity to become Briggs's puppet/judge?

"Do the honorable thing before it's too late," Jesse advised.

The man's eyes narrowed. "How dare you presume to tell me what to do?"

Jesse debated on how to play his hand. Should he show all his cards now in the hopes of stopping the trial before it began, or save his big guns for his defense?

Caution hadn't been his strong suit since he'd met Trinity. He'd go for broke.

"I don't know what hold Briggs has on you, but it better be worse than having to answer to Governor Adams."

"The governor isn't involved in this matter."

"Oh, but he is, and has been." Pain knotted in Jesse's chest like always when he thought about Jacob. "Briggs ordered my brother killed, and I've been watching him and reporting his activities to the governor for months."

Judge Pettibone's complexion turned green as brackish water.

"The covert work has been fascinating," Jesse rambled on, enjoying the other man's discomfort. "And the skills they taught us in criminology class have been invaluable. I had complete access to Mr. Briggs's private office and safe. Do you know about the land swindle, Judge? The tax evasion. The men and women he's rounded up and sold like cattle—sometimes across state lines. Not to mention the execution of two people."

The seawater color drained from the judge's face leaving him bleached white as the belly of a brook trout caught in receding water.

"It's true I was present at two stage holdups," Jesse admitted, "during which no one was injured. And the money I acquired was exchanged for marked bills. Funny how they found their way into Mr. Briggs's office."

"What about the woman to which the sheriff referred?"

"She's alive and well. Although I believe another woman did meet her death at Mr. Briggs's bidding."

The judge stepped backward as if he'd been physically assaulted.

Clavin straighten up and came to attention.

Judge Pettibone collected his composure. "Your statements have been duly noted." He signaled for Langford. "Take the prisoner to his cell."

"I might be the one in jail," Jesse called over his shoulder, "but you're the one who's trapped, Judge."

The sheriff shoved Jesse sideways into a wall, then muscled him out the door.

****

What was keeping his honor?

Mr. Briggs lounged in the over-stuffed chair and glanced around the dimly lit antechamber situated behind the altar. Being in a church generally made him uncomfortable, but he felt rather at home in this little parish, as if he were in charge not God Almighty. And like a displeased deity, Briggs was about to unleash his wrath.

The judge had performed poorly today, a matter which must be dealt with immediately. And Jesse Smith—or Callahan as it were—had been up to much more sabotage than he'd imagined. It had never occurred to him Jesse was Jacob Callahan's brother.

Briggs bit off the end of his cigar and spit the turd-like tidbit onto the floor.

He was beginning to regret the trial, and regrets always boded ill.

And then there were the girls to deal with. The traitorous whores would have to pay too—and not just in dollars. He'd sell them off in the mountains like the rest of the women and start over.

As the room edged toward darkness, Briggs's mood shifted from angry to vengeful and he waited silently—a rattler ready to strike. His prey should be arriving soon. Ah, here he was now.

Judge Pettibone rushed in, closed the door, and with a sigh leaned back against the smooth wood. Briggs struck a match to light his cigar. His quarry jumped and squinted in his direction. The flickering glow of yellow highlighted the judge's already jaundiced complexion.

"What are you going to do about this situation, Reggie?"

The Judge hurried to light the kerosene lamp. Sweat glistened on his upper lip and his hand shook as he poured himself a tumbler of water from the pitcher on the nearby desk. "There's nothing I can do," he said, with surprising conviction.

"Wrong answer, judge. Try again."

Water slopped from the glass as the judge raised it to his lips to take a swallow. "It's one thing for me to make sure a defendant is sentenced to hang once the jury finds him guilty, and quite another matter to overrule a jury's verdict, or railroad a lawyer. You can see I don't have the authority for such blatant twisting of the law."

"I can see you don't have the guts for the job."

The judge flinched and set the glass aside.

"Thanks to me, you live high off the hog, Reggie. It would be a shame to see you reduced to eating sowbelly again. And need I remind you of all the girls I've sent to warm your bed on your visits to Prairie Ridge. I even took care of the one you somehow managed to get pregnant."

"I didn't ask you to kill her, only send her away and keep her quiet."

"There's nothing more silent than the grave." Briggs leaned back in his chair.

"But the man knows legal procedure. He'll rip a hole wider than the state of Texas through our case. And he says there are records—on you and on Billy. Maybe even on me. Not to mention documents detailing his findings about the land swindles, and the kidnapping and selling of those men and women. I warned you to stay clear of that business."

Son of a bitch. Briggs chomped down on the end of his cigar. Callahan must have been playing him for months. Had Jesse found the journal secreted away in the vase? "He's bluffing. Where's the proof?"

"The details are all written down and on their way to the governor's office in Denver."

"No doubt the mission of that meddlesome newspaper man. I wondered where he'd disappeared to." If Jacob Callahan was Jesse's brother, then the old man was his uncle. It all made sense now. Briggs waved the smoldering cigar in the air. "The way the river's running, that ink-stained old bastard will be lucky to get there at all, let alone back here in time to make a difference."

"But the trial could go on for days."

"It could, but it won't."

"It's out of my hands. I can't promise anything."

"I was afraid you would say that, Reggie."

Now Briggs saw what needed to be done. It was simple really, and after all, wasn't that the key to success? Keeping things simple.

"Tomorrow, you will orchestrate the illusion of a trial with the defendant in absentia. The facts no longer matter. You make sure the jury finds Jesse Callahan guilty, and I'll make sure he hangs."

"Now see here—"

"No, you see here," Briggs warned. "The verdict is already in, the defendant has been found guilty, and the sentence shall be carried out in full—and quickly."

Chapter Twenty-Four

A savage punch caught Jesse hard in the stomach. He doubled over with pain and fought for a decent breath. This was a hell of a way to start the morning. When they dragged him from his cell to Briggs's office, he knew things had taken a turn for the worse.

The deputies jerked him upright, and Clavin hit him again, this time in the face. The sound of bone crunching registered in his mind, but he didn't know if it was his cheek or Clavin's knuckles. His left eye began swelling shut, and he never saw the blow that sent him reeling to the rough edge of darkness.

They released the death grip on his arms, and he crumpled to the carpeted floor. Rolling onto his side, he spit and coughed and tried not to choke on his own blood.

"Ready to talk yet?" Briggs asked.

The despicable little man peered down from where he perched on the edge of his polished desk. Jesse held his position and glared back at him. He could barely see straight, let alone talk, and even if he could utter a sentence, he wouldn't. Let Briggs sweat. Let him stew and wonder. It was small consolation but all he had to cling to at the moment.

Head down on the thick, soft rug, Jesse rallied his strength for the next round.

Briggs slid from the desk and stepped nearer.

"Perhaps you've forgotten the question."

Briggs stood so close, Jesse could smell bootblack and see the fancy side stitching on the hand-tooled leather boot disappearing up Briggs's trouser leg. How could such a small man harbor so much evil?

"I know you found the ledger. What other documents are heading to Denver?" Briggs slammed the toe of his boot into Jesse's ribs.

Rolling away from the pain, he clenched his jaw to stop the inhuman sound threatening to burst from his mouth. Faces and feelings danced through his brain, but they were fleeting shadows without substance, and he drew neither strength nor comfort from the confused montage.

A boot gouged into the soft part of Jesse's back, shoving his kidney to a place where it had no business being. He'd be pissing blood for a week if he lived that long. He gritted his teeth until he feared they might shatter.

Why didn't they just shoot him and get it over with?

The deputies dragged him upright to his knees.

"You're every bit as stubborn and nosey as your brother," Briggs snarled in his face. "Those characteristics are a deadly combination. And that same sense of useless honor is going to see you in a grave as well."

Jesse raised his head and glared up at Briggs, mustering enough strength to speak. "I'm not just Jacob Callahan's brother. I stand for every woman you've ever drugged, raped, and beaten. And I'm the voice of every man you've swindled and ordered to be killed."

Briggs tugged at his necktie as if the cloth was

suddenly too tight, and a haunted expression crept across his face. "You're insane," he snapped. "And I'm through asking questions. Get him out of here and lock him in the storeroom.

"When you're done," Briggs added, "one of you go to the livery. Hitch up the old stagecoach Willis keeps there and bring it around back."

"We goin' somewhere, boss?" At the idea, Clavin sounded as excited as a child.

"Yes. Indeed, we are." Briggs rubbed his hands together as if in anticipation. "But first, I've a mind for a good, hearty breakfast."

****

Jesse squinted at the sunlight spearing through the cracks in the boarded-up windows. Even those small shards of white light burned a path straight to the back of his brain.

Damn—he'd been thrown from and stomped on by a horse and felt more optimistic about living than he felt right now.

With a groan, he sat up and leaned against a crate of wine. Pain ricocheted through his head and nausea crawled around his stomach. Thankfully, the cut above his eye had stopped oozing and the taste of blood no longer permeated his mouth.

Skimming his tongue across his cracked and swollen lips, he glanced around. Briggs had made some improvements since the last time he'd been in the storeroom. With the windows reinforced, the room was sturdier than a Kansas root cellar.

Guarding his ribs with one hand, he dragged himself upright with the other. He'd always imagined lawyering would be more dignified and less painful than this. He waited for his vision to clear and the blood to reach his brain.

Trying not to jostle his battered body, he hunched over and walked as if on eggshells, crossing the room to the door. He jiggled the knob—locked—of course.

With his back to the wood, he slid to the floor. His stomach growled. He'd been evicted from his cell and hustled to the office before sunup and breakfast. Why hadn't they just beaten him up at the jail?

There seemed little doubt the trial would be quick and ruled in their favor. The judge had crossed the line, and Jesse knew how easily that could happen. For a while, bitterness and vengeance had taken the place of all his other emotions. He'd welcomed the seduction of the dark side as he romanced the danger and courted the enemy. He'd momentarily forgotten the good side of life, the joyous part celebrating everyday existence. Trinity had pulled him back from the abyss, saving him from becoming a part of what he fought against.

A scuffling sounded at the door.

"Hey, Mr. Callahan, you in there?"

The revelation of his real name had spread quickly. Jesse hitched around and peered through the keyhole. A child's bright clear blue eye stared back at him. It was Laughing Kate's son. Jesse had seen him around the place a few times. They'd talked once about horses and Cheyenne Indians.

"That you, Petey?"

"Yeah. What's goin' on?" Petey's voice held high-pitched curiosity.

Jesse turned back around and slumped against the wall. "How did you know I was here?" he asked, avoiding the boy's question.

"One of the men was braggin' to the girls about the beating they give you. When he finally left, ma told me to find out how you were. You hurt bad?"

"I've felt worse, but I can't remember when. How'd you manage to sneak past Briggs's boys?'

"I'm just like the dog." Petey sounded matter-of-fact. "Nobody pays me no mind. If I stick to the shadows and don't get underfoot, I can go anywhere I like."

A dubious honor to be as invisible as a mongrel pup. "See if you can unlock the door from your side."

Petey responded with louder than anticipated enthusiasm.

"Easy boy," Jesse called. "Try to keep the racket to a minimum."

"Sorry. It's locked real good. I could fetch some dynamite or somethin' and come back." Little boy enthusiasm accompanied his words.

Jesse smiled. Everything was an adventure when you were Petey's age. "Thanks anyway, partner. I'm sure I'll be fine right here until the trial resumes. Now you better light a shuck and skedaddle. If you get caught talking to me, you'll be in big trouble."

"But I want to help," Petey pleaded.

"Then you can start by doing what you're told." He hoped his tone was harsh enough to get his point across. "And that goes for your mother and the other girls. The way you can all help me most is to stay out of harm's way."

Silence followed.

Maybe if the kid had something to look forward to, he'd follow orders now. "When this is over," Jesse promised, "you and me and Webster will spend a day together in the country. I'll teach you how to ride and rope."

"Can I shoot your pistol too?"

Jesse shook his head. No matter where you found them, little boys were all the same. "Maybe the rifle. Every man should know how to defend his family and hunt for food. Now git. And don't forget to tell your mother to stay away."

"Yes, sir, Mr. Callahan. And I won't forget your promise neither."

"Me too, Petey."

"I knew Jacob. He was a good man."

Petey's words took him by surprise and brought a lump to his throat.

"Yes. He was. Now git."

He thought he heard the child scurry away, but he leaned around to check through the keyhole anyway. The alleyway was empty.

He thought about the promise to Petey and laughed. The only thing Webster hated more than fidgety females was a calamitous kid. He'd have to buy the roan a new bridle as payment—one with silver conchos. The darn horse's vanity was second only to his loyalty.

Why the tarnation was he even worrying? His chance of spending a peaceful day in the country any time soon was slim to none, and slim was riding out of town on a fast horse.

A new set of footsteps echoed beyond the door. The long stride and ponderous rhythm sounded like Clavin's. Jesse crawled away from the panel, gained his feet, and leaned against a tower of whiskey barrels.

A key turned in the lock and the door swung open.

It was him, the colossus. Rhodes had Helios and Prairie Ridge had Clavin.

"Time to go," the big man ordered.

"Go where?" Jesse hoped for a clue as to what Briggs had in mind.

"Go where I tell you," the giant chortled. The guileless quality of Clavin's laugh was unnerving. "Now," the man ordered, brandishing a pistol. The other side of his personality was equally as unhinged.

In an attempt to avoid a muzzle-prodding, Jesse tried to keep his gait steady and his path unswerving as he headed out the door.

"This way." Clavin clamped a hand the size of a bear's paw on Jesse's shoulder, propelling him to the right.

A chill snaked across his shoulders when he saw the old stagecoach waiting. Briggs sat inside, calmly smoking a cigar. A team was hitched and ready to go. But go where? Not to the jail or back to the court room. He had a bad feeling about this.

Jesse took a step sideways. They hadn't replaced his leg irons or the wrist manacles. Maybe he should make a break for freedom. He tensed his muscles, ready to run.

"Not so fast, your lawyership." The sheriff materialized at his side, along with two henchmen. A hollow thud rang out as they slammed him up against the side of stagecoach and bound his wrists with whipcord.

Jesse glanced wildly around. Petey was the only one in sight, sitting at the top of the stairs leading to the bordello.

Clavin lumbered up and into the driver's seat.

Langford opened the stagecoach door. Jesse's right shoulder scraped along the framework as the deputies tossed him inside. Pitching headfirst to the far side of the coach, he landed on the floor across from Briggs.

"Does Judge Pettibone know about this?"

"Judge Pettibone is conducting your trial as we speak. The verdict being obvious, we're going to carry out the sentencing."

Mounting the waiting horses, the deputies took up position around the coach.

Briggs stuck his head out one window, signaling to Langford. "Make sure all the good citizens of Prairie Ridge are gathered in the church for the trial. Then we'll slip out of town by the back way."

Dread formed a fiery ball in Jesse's stomach, burning like the rotgut whiskey Briggs sold. The trial was nothing but a diversion. He'd given the judge the opportunity to do the right thing, but the man not only hadn't seen the light, he'd sought greater darkness as a refuge.

"You got it, boss." The sheriff nodded and heaved a coil of rope inside the coach.

The weighty bundle landed on Jesse's chest, the coarse loops slapping against his cheek, his bruised ribs screaming with renewed agony. Shrugging off the hemp, he swallowed hard. One end was fashioned into a hangman's noose.

Chapter Twenty-Five

Running late, Trinity headed for the church. Whether Jesse liked it or not, she would be there ready to speak up if things went wrong. She should have done so yesterday.

"Psst. Miss Trinity." She froze and glanced around. "Over here."

Kate's son, Petey, beckoned from the shadows, the usual grin missing from his freckled face. Reaching the lad, she crouched at his side and slipped one arm around his shoulders. "Petey, what is it?"

"Jesse's in big trouble."

"I know, Petey. But his trial is about to start. Things may still go his way."

"No, you don't understand. They took him."

"What do you mean? Who took him?"

She straightened, trying not to panic.

"Come on, I'll show you."

They hurried across the side street and to the alley at the back entrance of the bordello.

"They were right here, honest. In an old stagecoach."

"Who was here, Petey? That's sounds like one of your fantastic stories."

"I swear I'm telling the truth. It was Mr. Briggs and Clavin and the sheriff and some other guys. They had Jesse tied up inside. I guess they left." Using the toe of his worn boot, he jabbed at the deep muddy ruts. "See, here's their tracks."

She studied the ground. "They left from here? Not from the jail?"

"Yes, ma'am. Jesse's been locked up in the small storeroom since sunup."

Dread channeled deeper into her thoughts. Maybe Petey was confused. "Are you sure they didn't take Jesse to the trial?" She had to ask, reaching for false hope.

"No, look at the tracks," he insisted. "The coach headed that way." He pointed in the opposite direction of the church.

"How long ago did they leave?"

He shrugged. "Just now, I guess, when I went to fetch you. But I reckon they might have some trouble along the way."

"Why is that?"

Petey grinned and retrieved two long, rusty carriage pins from his pants pocket.

Trinity smiled. "That was wonderfully ingenious," she said, "and daring. It might buy Jesse some precious time."

"I like Mr. Smith, I mean Mr. Callahan." Petey returned the hardware to his pocket. "He's gonna teach me to ride and rope. Leastwise he said he would. Is he a man to keep his promises?"

Pride and love quickened within her like new life. "Yes. He won't let you down." Not if they could reach him in time.

She studied the backdoor at the top of the stairs. She could try shooting through from this side, but that would be a noisy affair. And surely Mr. Briggs had left someone guarding his property—which included the girls. She'd try the street entrance.

"Follow me, Petey." She tightened her grip on her purse, reassured by the weight of big Colt revolver, and led the way around to the front of the building. Oddly, there was no ruffian stationed out front. She pushed her way through the swinging doors, Petey in tow.

"Wait here." She ushered him to one side. He nodded and faded into the shadows.

The dimly lit gambling hall was silent, but the smell of men, liquor, and smoke still hovered in the air—diluted remnants of last night's tomfooleries.

A tall, thin, disagreeable-looking man leaned against the bar, nursing a half-empty glass of what looked like whiskey. She didn't see anyone else.

Armed with a smile and spurred on by a galloping heartbeat, Trinity sashayed in the man's direction. He was wearing a gun, and the hilt of a knife showed above his left boot top.

He glanced up, set his drink aside, and openly leered at her.

She fought the urge to wipe at her face and chest as his prurient gaze dripped down the front of her body like a layer of slime.

"We're closed, missy."

She paused several steps beyond his reach. "Oh please. Might I just have a sip of water or a sarsaparilla? I feel so decidedly warm." She fluttered her eyelashes, although based on his prior interest, the ploy seemed unnecessary.

"Well now," he said, hiking up his trousers, "maybe something could be arranged."

"I'll be more than happy to pay for the drink." She

pretended to fumble in her purse for coinage. "I'm sure this will cover the cost."

Sliding the Colt free, she leveled it at the man's chest.

His smile faded. "That thing loaded?"

She cocked the hammer back. "There's one sure way to find out."

"Now hold on there." He eased away from the bar—hands out in front of his body as if he could ward off a slug from a forty-five. "You just calm down, little lady."

Trinity was in no mood to be patronized. "You'll be dead calm in two seconds if you don't do exactly as I say. Do you understand?"

"Yes," he squawked, all but choking on the one syllable, his gaze locked onto the muzzle of the pistol.

"Good. Take off your gun belt and lay it on that table next to you. Then put the boot-knife you're toting with it. When you're done, get your hands in the air and back away."

He just stood there and stared at her as if he'd been turned to stone.

"You've got two choices, mister. You can either get a move on or sing soprano at the next Sunday Social." She lowered the muzzle until it was pointing at his crotch.

He followed her orders, and his hands shook as he raised them and stepped back.

"That's more like it." She tightened her two-fisted grip on the heavy revolver. "Petey. Go get your mom and the other women."

The boy materialized at her side. "They're locked in. I tried earlier."

"Give Petey the key, mister. Now."

Petey darted forward to accept the prize, then he ran off to set them all free.

What next? She couldn't stand here all day watching this yahoo. "Take off your clothes," she ordered, "starting with your boots and trousers."

He hesitated. "Mind if I step behind the bar?"

"Shyness doesn't become you. You're fine where you are."

Unmoving he returned her glare.

Damn. All she wanted was to get out of here and go find Jesse.

"Oh, do what you want," she finally gave in. "Just hurry it up."

He smirked and turned away—suddenly all too eager to please.

"Hold it," she snapped.

He jerked to a halt his hands still in the air.

Keeping the pistol trained on his chest, she circled around and preceded him to the backside of the bar. On the top shelf, beneath the smooth expanse of polished wood, lay a double barrel shotgun.

Sweat trickled down between her breasts as she realized just how close she'd come to having her head blown off.

"You sneaky little weasel." Too angry to be afraid of the unfamiliar weapon, she snatched up the gun with her free hand and slammed it down on top of the bar.

The man sidestepped away from the business end of the barrels. "Can't kill a man for tryin'," he sneered.

"Oh yes I can, and next time I will." The anger and injustice of a lifetime seemed concentrated in her words, and taking note, he started pulling off his boots and pants as if his clothes were on fire.

Before long, the rush of footsteps and women's voices filled the silence.

"Oh look, girls," Mary June trilled. "Party favors." She claimed the holster and revolver.

Kate reached for the boot knife. It went well with the black whip she'd thought to bring along.

Annie retrieved the shotgun. Thankfully she handled it as if she knew how to use one. The other girls circled around—one recovered two more pistols from behind the bar.

Heady with relief, Trinity lowered her weapon. Then she nudged a chair into a corner.

"Have a seat, mister."

Annie reinforced the request with a wave of the shotgun.

Barefooted and clothed in a filthy, threadbare union suit, the man gingerly took to the chair.

Catching on fast, two other women retrieved twists of gold cord holding back the nearby red drapery. One bound his wrists, and the other secured his upper body to the back of the chair.

Mary June stepped closer. "Well if it isn't Dunstan, our not-so-friendly watchdog. What's the matter, honey? You look like you don't know whether to take a piss or get a hard on."

The girls hooted.

"Go to hell," he rasped.

"Been there," Mary June said, "thanks to men like you."

Trinity poked a finger at his chest. "Where'd they take Jesse?"

"I ain't tellin' you nothin'," he snarled. "Briggs'd

kill me if I open my mouth."

Trinity fumed at his obstinacy. She didn't have time for a battle of wills. "Maybe he will, maybe he won't. But one thing is for sure, I'll kill you now if you don't."

Dunstan remained silent, calling her bluff. And unfortunately that was pretty much what it was.

Kate stepped forward. "I hear you roughed up my kid the other day when he wouldn't fetch you tobacco from the general store."

"He deserved it. The little shit. He ain't nothin' but a whore's mistake.

"He's no mistake, but you just made one." Retrieving a lit kerosene lamp, Kate ambled toward the obstinate man

"What are you doing?" He kicked at her and wrenched at the ties binding him in place.

"Now don't move about," Kate said sweetly, "you might accidently get burned." Placing the brass base on his head, she balanced the lamp in the corner where the walls met behind him. Then stepping to the bar, she grabbed two bottles of hard liquor, and returned to his side.

"Try your question again, Trinity."

"Where did Briggs take Jesse?"

"I don't know."

Kate dashed the bottle of tequila to the hardwood floor. The flammable liquid and shards of glass splattered Dunstan's bare feet and the legs of his union suit.

"You crazy bitch," he shrieked. When the lamp trembled, he gasped in alarm and stopped thrashing about.

"Where did Mr. Briggs take Jesse?" Trinity repeated.

"They're headed for Becker's hollow, just east of town," he blurted.

"How many men are with Briggs?"

"I don't remember."

Uncorking the second bottle, Kate poured whiskey over Dunstan's chest and privates, soaking the front of his gruesome long johns.

"If that lantern falls, you'll go up quicker than a corn stalk in late November." Mary June took a step back as if expecting flames to erupt.

Dunstan rolled his eyes like a crazed animal and made a strangling noise before he spoke. "Clavin's with Briggs, and there's the sheriff, and at least two others. They're gonna do a little rope stretchin'. I swear that's all I know."

It took a moment for her to realize what he meant. Then the horrible image reeled through Trinity's mind, and she thought she was going to be sick.

Mary June laid a hand on her arm. "We'll get there in time," she promised. "But we need horses. We can stop at the livery on the way out of town."

"I'll slip over to the stable ahead of you," Lolly volunteered, heading toward the door. "Willis has a thing for me. I'll keep him busy until you're all safely on your way."

"Thank you, Lolly." Mary June handed one of the extra weapons to Camille. "You and the rest of the girls hold down the fort and keep a good eye on Dunstan. And be careful. Stay on your toes in case they bring Jesse back here for some reason.

"*Mais oui.*" Camille nodded. "We shall keep the

home fires burning."

At the word fire, Dunstan shuddered and rolled his eyes.

Kate kept the knife but happily took the other revolver Mary June offered up.

Trinity's gaze flickered over the girls. Then a flash of wonderment shot through her. These women were brave and loyal and willing to stand with her against all odds. They were more than just friends—they were like a family.

They were also all half naked.

Outfitted in ribbons and lace, wearing audacious camisoles and daring ruffled petticoats, they were an unabashed assortment of thighs and cleavage, decked out more for riding bed-rails than dirt trails. "You can't go dressed like that," Trinity ventured. "You'll catch your death...or something."

"I'm afraid it'll have to do," Annie said. "Mr. Briggs took all our other clothes."

"Not to worry," Mary June said and grinned. "Half the men in the county have seen us wearin' less." She strapped the gun belt around her red corset, tugging a frill of black lace down over the leather.

Rebellion glowed in her eyes. "Come along, ladies," she encouraged, patting a curl into place. "It's time to break a few heads instead of hearts."

Chapter Twenty-Six

Trinity kicked at the horse with her heels and made clucking noises, but her attempts seemed to annoy Webster rather than spur him to greater action.

She knew the gelding could run like a buck deer, yet he lumbered along at a snail's pace. How was she going to rescue Jesse when she couldn't even get out of town?

Now he wandered off into a patch of cow parsnip. She yanked on the reins, but the big roan shook his head and reached farther forward, almost dragging her from the saddle. Fear tightened into a hard lump in her stomach. Jesse was going to die because she couldn't outsmart a horse.

"Leave that ornery critter here and ride with me," Mary June suggested.

Trinity considered the idea. Other than Webster, there had only been two other saddle horses in the livery. Mary June had one, and Annie and Kate rode double on the other. To relinquish another mount seemed a poor choice.

"A complement of two is hardly intimidating. And it makes us a more concentrated target."

"That makes sense," Mary June agreed, gently retrieving a ladybug trying to crawl down her cleavage.

Besides, being with Webster made Trinity feel closer to Jesse, giving her strength, making her less afraid of what might be waiting up ahead. And if the worst happened, they would need a horse to carry Jesse back to town.

But how did you reason with twelve hundred pounds of uncooperative horseflesh? Furious, Trinity slid to the ground and grabbed Webster's bridle. "Now listen up, you stubborn son of a plow-horse. Jesse needs us."

The horse reared back, but she held tight, wrestling his head down until she could look him in the eye. Tears slid down her cheeks and dropped onto Webster's silky muzzle. "I can't do this alone. I love him too, you know." The gelding snorted in surprise, inhaling the crystal droplets.

"Please," she sobbed. "You have to trust me." Her face was so close to the horse, their breath mingled. Then their gazes locked, and he whickered and gave her a gentle nudge. Taking the hint, she mounted up. Barely in the saddle, reins in hand, the gelding leaped forward.

Clinging to the saddle horn, Trinity tore past her friends. At their collective "Yahoo", she dared to glance back over her shoulder.

Amidst a flurry of ribbon and lace, the girls hurried to catch up.

****

The coach jarred over a rut. Still lying on the floor, Jesse's head slammed against the door. He hunched over to one side to avoid a second blow then shifted around trying to relieve the pain riddling his battered body.

Briggs stared out the window with seeming disinterest.

The sheriff leaned forward. "Quit rootin' around,"

217

he ordered. "We'll be there soon enough. Then the only thing you'll have to worry about is a quick pain in your neck." He gave a twisted grin and relaxed back against the tattered velvet seat.

Jesse stared at the rope. They were going to get away with murder—again. And everything he had hoped for and believed in was going to die with him. There would be nobody left in Prairie Ridge to stop Briggs. He would devour the last vestiges of freedom the town possessed and feed upon the sorrows of the people at his leisure.

Worst of all, the woman he loved and the women at the bordello would be left to Briggs's mercy. Trinity Tuesday might have known trouble before, but nothing like this. And he wouldn't be there to protect her—just as he hadn't been there to save Jacob.

As the coach careened over the storm-ravaged road, the past collided with the future, and disjointed thoughts tumbled through his mind. He closed his eyes and saw Jacob's face, at age six, twelve, eighteen—then imagined in death. He might be joining his brother soon.

Before Jacob's death, he'd never thought twice about growing old. And after Jacob was gone, nothing really seemed to matter. He opened his eyes, and recollections of a young woman with a defiant expression and a temper that wouldn't concede to fear replaced the images of horror.

He'd imagined the years he would spend with Trinity, building a home, raising kids, doing their part to lead this half-tamed, defiant nation into a new era. They would have years together to love one another, to learn about and from one another. Now those years may never come.

Almost worse than the idea of dying was the idea of dying without ever telling Trinity how much he loved her. How had he allowed that to happen?

If he got out of this alive, he would tell Trinity how he felt and drive the loneliness from her heart. Replace whatever nightmare she'd run from with memories they would forge together.

He had to tell Trinity he loved her. He chanted the words over and over in his mind, a litany keeping time with the rhythm of hoof beats and the sway of the coach. And one way or another, he had to stop Briggs.

The floorboards vibrated violently. Then the undercarriage rattled and creaked unnaturally, culminating in the sound of splintering wood. Instinctively Jesse lodged one foot up against the opposite door.

The coach lurched from side to side. He could hear Clavin up-top cursing and wrestling the team as the horses whinnied in fear. Next, it felt as if they'd dipped into a muddy runoff on the side of the road. The forward momentum ceased abruptly. The coach continued to hover upright for a moment before pitching off to one side.

A deputy's face appeared in the out-of-kilter window. "The axle's come lose on the near side," he reported, "and we lost a spoke off the wheel."

Cursing under his breath, Briggs grabbed the frame of the window and pulled himself upright. "Can it be repaired?"

The man disappeared from view and Jesse heard voices deliberating.

"It's possible," the returning man said. "Won't

know for sure until we get under there. But…"

"But what? Get on with it."

The deputy hesitated and cleared his throat. "It would hurry things along if you all were to wait out here." He stepped back as if expecting repercussions for the suggestion.

Apparently, Briggs wasn't in the mood for shooting messengers today. "You heard the man. Everybody out."

Langford jumped to open the door and assist his employer out of the teetering vehicle. Then he kicked Jesse in the leg. "You too."

Jesse managed to scoot, roll, and crawl out the door, then gain his feet.

"Stand over there." Langford nodded toward the road. "Stay in plain sight, and don't try nothin'. Don't even breathe heavy."

Standing in the middle of the dirt lane, Jesse studied his surroundings. The mid-morning sun struggle to burst through the clouds but lost the fight. Were they in for more rain? He wondered if Sol had been able to cross the river and make it to Denver.

Briggs picked his way through the underbrush, lounged against a fallen log, and lit a fresh cigar. "Be quick about it, men," he mandated, "but make sure the repairs are solid." Pausing he blew a smoke ring in the air. "After hanging a man, it makes good sense to have reliable transportation at the ready when taking one's leave."

Jesse worked the kinks from his shoulder muscles. This was probably his best chance to get away. A cold calm settled over him, and a strength he would have sworn had been beaten out of him pumped through his veins.

The drainage was better on the left side of the road, and the terrain appeared dryer. He would leave less of a trail in that direction. It would be rough going with his hands tied. But if he made it to the trees without being shot, he might have a chance. He shifted his gaze back to the men.

Clavin grunted, his face turning crimson as he strained to lift the lopsided coach while two other men forced the mended wheel back onto the realigned axle. Then they commenced pounding and hammering underneath the vehicle.

Langford drew closer to inspect the repair work. Apparently satisfied, he reached inside and retrieved the thick coil of rope. "Ready when you are, Mr. Briggs."

Jesse spun around and broke for the woods.

Over the rush of air in his lungs and the crunch of sand and pebbles beneath his boots, he swore he heard the hammer being cocked back on Langford's pistol. He ran faster.

Something whizzed by his ear as the sound of gunfire split the air. Then another shot rang out. Jesse stumbled, caught himself, and clenched his jaw waiting for the pain. None came. Raising his bound wrists before him, he dodged two scrub oaks and leaped over small sagebrush.

The sound of men approaching on foot clawed at his back. The two deputies might be short on brains, but they were long on legs.

The younger one dove into him, taking Jesse down.

He hit the ground hard, a sharp rock gouging his hip as he rolled to one side. Before he could shake off the dirt, they hauled him upright, and the sheriff backhanded him across the face. He staggered and fought to keep his balance.

Coarse hemp scraped along the side of his face and tore at his ear as they settled the prickly noose around his neck. Pushing and shoving, the three men hustled him back toward the stagecoach—and a sturdy cottonwood.

Briggs reached inside the coach and retrieved a basket and a bottle of wine. Then casually as you please, he perched in the open doorway of the conveyance. With a chicken leg in one hand and a glass of wine in the other, he appeared as happy as a kid at the circus waiting for the main event.

Coiling the far end of the rope, Langford tossed it over a thick limb, and yanked it tight.

Jesse stood three inches taller and gasped for a decent breath.

"Bring a stump over here," the sheriff ordered.

A deputy loped off to do his bidding.

Jesse's eyes burned from more than the rope choking him. Blinking fast, he tried to think of a parting comment to fling in Briggs's face, but couldn't. Only Trinity came to mind, and he reckoned that's the way it should be. If he had to leave this world, her image was what he wanted to carry into the next. Take care of her, Sol.

The stump was set in place, but before they forced him to step up, a rumbling sounded in the distance. There were horses approaching—at a gallop.

The sheriff heard it too. He dropped the rope, and everyone turned toward the road they'd just come down. Whoever was coming was hidden by the convoluted terrain.

Was it Sol? If so, he'd made it back in the nick of time.

Hope and anticipation thumped in Jesse's chest. Hands still tied in front of his body, he shed the noose and edged around the tree.

Three horses crested the rise, mud flying from their hooves as they charged down the embankment. They were firing wildly, sending the sheriff and his men running for cover. As the riders galloped closer, flashes of pink, red, and baby blue pierced the confusion.

Definitely not Sol with reinforcements. He squeezed his eyes shut and looked again.

They were women, and Trinity was at the head of the pack—riding Webster no less. They carried weapons, but even well-armed, a good outcome seemed unlikely.

"Hold your fire, men." Briggs laughed so hard he nearly unseated himself. "I'll be damned, if it isn't a candy-assed posse of pulchritude."

Chapter Twenty-Seven

A bullet slammed into the coach two inches from Briggs's head, quickly changing his attitude. The smile faded from his face as he lunged to the ground. "Shoot back, you fools," he ordered, crawling off to one side.

The men came alive, and with pistols raised, they took aim.

Jesse ran and dropped to the ground on the far side of the coach. Amongst the blur of petticoats and garters he recognized the other riders as Mary June, Kate, and Annie. Fire blazed from their eyes, and their red painted lips held no seductive smiles. They thundered past, sending the men scrambling for cover. But guts and determination wouldn't turn aside bullets.

Gaining his feet, Jesse released the brake on the coach and urged the team forward until the stage traversed the road at an angle. Then he reset the brake leaving the conveyance as a barrier between the women and the gunmen who were firing off several rounds.

The women replied with a heated volley—one of the deputies went down. Legs furiously pumping, Briggs scrambled farther into the underbrush. The armed men spread out, seeking defensive positions behind rocks and trees.

One man lagged behind. Creeping forward, Jesse head-butted his opponent, sending the man crashing to the ground. A swift kick to the head kept him there.

Commandeering the man's revolver, Jesse rolled to the side and slid into the side gully running the length of the road.

The smell of gunpowder and the neighs of frightened horses filled the air. The women regrouped on this side of the coach. Plunging and kicking, the frightened team broke loose, leaving the stage stranded crosswise in the road.

Kate caught Jesse's eye. Risking all, she drew closer and aimed the knife she carried in his direction. The blade found its mark about a foot from his shoulder, buried up to the hilt in the sandy ground. He was glad the girls were on his side. As they retreated out of pistol range, he prayed they wouldn't try another frontal attack.

Retrieving the knife, he cut the ropes binding his wrists. Then he counted heads. There were three men missing. One was the deputy the girls took out, and one was the man he'd knocked unconscious. The other was the sheriff.

He glanced around the surrounding countryside. A movement in the tall grass caught his attention. The law-dog was circling around trying to outflank the women. From this angle they'd never see him.

Gauging the distance to the women, Jesse gained his feet, and ran like the devil. Bullets whizzed past his head and dug into the ground at his feet. He jagged to the left, then the right, feeling the breathy kiss of death with each bounding step he took.

When the girls saw him, they misinterpreted his purpose, and headed his way.

"Go back," Jesse yelled, but they rode all the faster, playing right into Langford's hands. All the coldhearted brute had to do was lay low and pick them off one at a time.

He pointed to the left, hoping they would see the man waiting to gun them down. They thought it was a signal and veered off in that direction. Sunlight reflected off the sheriff's gun as he rose up and leveled his sights. Jesse motioned frantically trying to alert the unsuspecting women of the danger. Then he begged God for a miracle—he might not deserve one, but they did.

In desperation he fired his own pistol, knowing he was too far away. The crack of a rifle shot split the chaos. But the sound didn't come from the sheriff's direction, for the man pitched forward out of the bushes and tumbled to the ground.

The girls' horses skidded to a halt—mud and rock splattering in all directions.

None of the women were toting rifles.

Jesse glanced over his shoulder.

On top of a nearby hill, a lone cavalry soldier stood in silhouette. He thrust his rifle into a saddle scabbard, and then raised a bugle to his lips. The call to charge followed, and a full complement of soldiers crested the hill behind the advance scout. This time it really was Sol, with a well-armed troop. But they were still a ways off.

Pistol at the ready, Mary June slid from her horse and edged toward the unmoving sheriff. Jesse motioned for Trinity, Kate, and Annie to stay where they were. Webster pranced sideways eager for more action. Trinity appeared pale as she leaned forward to stroke the big gelding's neck. Her touch seemed to calm the beast—like master, like horse.

A glorious sight, the soldiers charged forward, rounding up Briggs's men in quick military fashion.

Sol directed his mount away from the melee and headed for Jesse.

Reining in his horse, the older man fought to catch his breath. "Thank the Lord you're all right, boy. I've been praying the whole way to Denver and back we wouldn't be too late."

"You arrived with the width of a gnat's eyelash to spare." Jesse grinned up at his uncle.

Sol glanced around, noting the hangman's noose hanging from the tree. "Where's Briggs? We've got arrest warrants from the governor for him and all his henchmen."

Jesse's smile faded when he spotted Briggs scurrying along an arroyo like the black-hearted varmint he was. "Keep the women out of my way." Still carrying the deputy's revolver, Jesse made for the ravine.

Wanting to remember every detail of Briggs's demise, Jesse forced himself not to hurry. As he advanced, he rotated the cylinder on the revolver and checked the load. Maybe he shouldn't want this so badly, but he did, and he wasn't ashamed to admit it to himself or Almighty God. He'd earned the right to avenge his brother's death. He'd earned the right to watch Briggs die.

Gaining ground with every step, he quickly overtook the little man. His quarry squealed like a pig as Jesse collared him from behind.

Placing one hand around Briggs's throat, Jesse pressed the muzzle of the pistol against the man's forehead with the other. The gratification was near intoxicating as he curled his finger around the trigger. This was it, his moment of triumph. His breath came in gasps, and pleasure flowed through him as he anticipated the release of all the hate churning in his gut.

"Jesse." He heard Trinity's voice and the rustle of her skirt as she reached his side. The tiny shimmer of sound washed over him, but he didn't look at her. She reached out. Did she think he should turn the other cheek—live and let live? Sometimes a man was pushed beyond proverbs. Sometimes a man had to make his own brand of justice.

Briggs squirmed like a toad and blinked his beady eyes—eyes bright with the knowledge his life was about to end. A life sustained on the pain and suffering of others.

Then Jesse was glad Trinity was here, because now what he was about to do, he did for her.

He tightened his grip and pulled the trigger.

Moisture spread over the front of Briggs's trousers as shrieking and blubbering he raised his hands, examining his body for holes. There were none.

Jesse let out a strangled groan, pulling the trigger repeatedly, churning up the earth around the coward trembling at his feet. In the end, he couldn't kill a man in cold blood, not even Briggs. And he wasn't about to sacrifice his future with Trinity for one brief moment of revenge—no matter how hard earned. Jacob wouldn't want him to either.

There had been a time when getting an eye for an eye was all he'd lived for. But times changed, and thanks to Trinity, so had he. For now, he'd have to be satisfied with seeing Briggs lying in a puddle of his own piss and fear. Let the murdering weasel wonder every minute of every day he spent waiting to hang why Jesse hadn't made it easy for him. Let Briggs scream useless threats at him every step of the way to the gallows.

A soldier hurried forward, prodded Briggs to his feet, and dragged him away.

"Allowing him to live was evermore courageous than shooting him." Trinity reached for Jesse and burrowed into his waiting embrace.

"The law will take care of Briggs, and I'm going to take care of you." He held her tight, curtailing the words of reprimand battling for release in the back of his throat. There would be time later to scold her for pulling such a stunt. Right now, he only wanted to tell her how much he loved her.

He eased her away from his chest, but no words came as he stared at the blood on his hand. Trinity's eyelids fluttered, and a shudder ran through her. Dear God—she'd been shot.

She touched his cheek with a trembling hand, and her lips curved into a weak smile as he swept her up into his arms. "We saved you." Then she went limp in his arms, and his heart seemed to stand still.

"You saved me, Trinity, even from myself."

Chapter Twenty-Eight

Sheriff Langford was dead. Briggs, Judge Pettibone, Billy Bart, and Clavin were all under arrest. And although still bedridden after a week, Trinity was making good progress.

According to the doctor, a full recovery should follow. He'd removed the bullet from Trinity's right side without difficulty, and although blood loss had been significant, he didn't think her liver had been damaged. Even with this reassurance, to see her pale as a ghost and lying abed in the brothel bridal suite, Jesse worried about her night and day.

When he wasn't at her side, Mary June or one of the other girls saw to her needs and made sure she ate. This morning was his turn.

"It's a bright, sunny day. Would you like to take a walk outside? Get some fresh air."

"I don't think so, Jesse. I want to stay here where I'm safe."

Being shot seemed to have affected Trinity's mind as well as her body. Usually fearless, she now seemed edgy, jumping at any unexpected noise, preferring to stay abed while the world passed her by. The full story as to why she'd run away had finally come out, and she'd told Mary June she would never feel out of danger as long as the Hatfields were searching for her.

Jesse couldn't make her heal any faster, but there

was one thing he could do to help her.

"All right then. You just rest and keep getting stronger. I have to go away for a few days."

"No." She reached for his hand, a troubled expression in her eyes.

"Everything is going to be all right. And so will you. Sol promised to come and read to you, and the girls are anxious to continue their lessons. I saw them dragging a chalk board as far as Mary June's room. I believe there is a secret plan in the works. Something about invading your room and demand your tutelage. You'll be so busy you won't even miss me."

That brought a momentary smile to her face. "Where are you going? I miss you already and you haven't even left."

"Just some unfinished business—to settle once and for all. And I have a surprise in mind for you, along with some grand ideas for the future. Now promise you'll do as you're told and take the medicine the doctor left for you."

"But it tastes awful."

"Yes, I imagine it does. That's why it's called medicine, and not served at Ladies' Tea."

****

Jesse hurried down the stairs to Mary June's room.

"And you're sure she said Middle Kiowa?" He reached for the note she held.

"Yes. The information is here on this paper. I sneaked it out of her hatbox. The woman has adjourning property to those wretched no-goods who raised her. And before you ask, yes, I'll be sure someone stays with her night and day. Just hurry. I think this is the only thing that will ease her mind and renew her fighting spirit.

"And by the by, you look like the devil's backside."

He gave a small burst of sorry laughter. "That would be an improvement over how I feel."

"A little hot food might help. According to Annie, you barely touched the tray she brought up last night. You're not doing Trinity any good by making yourself sick."

Mary June was correct. He'd stop at Sol's on the way out of town and beg some food.

****

"But you said he was back, Mary June. He's been gone for days and I'm anxious to see him."

"I know, honey, but you're to stay put until he comes for you. Are you hungry? You should try to eat something."

"No," Trinity said, throwing aside the covers. "All I need is Jesse."

Mary June pushed her back down onto the mattress. "Oh, no, you don't. You're staying put. Jesse would skin me alive if I let you up. It's real important that for once you follow his orders."

Trinity slumped against the pillows. Getting past Mary June was going to take some cunning. "All right," she agreed. "I'll be good, and I would like some broth and a biscuit."

Mary June's face brightened, and she hurried to the door. "I'll be back with the food directly."

As her friend's footsteps died away, Trinity swung her legs over the edge of the bed and sat up. Waiting for her surroundings to shift back into place, she glanced around. Everything appeared bright and new as if it had just been painted and polished. The whole world seemed dazzling after her previous weakness and narrow escape from death. But it also seemed dangerous.

Hugging herself for warmth, she shuffled across the room and opened the door to the wardrobe. Putting on a dress sounded like it would be a monumental effort. Instead she grabbed a cloak and slipped the warm wool on over her nightdress.

Where were her shoes? She couldn't find her shoes. She didn't care—she had to see Jesse.

Barefoot, she padded down the steps leading to the rooms behind the saloon. Then she followed the sound of Jesse's voice to the anteroom reserved for private parties. There were other voices coming from the parlor too—horrible, familiar voices—ones that had scarred her past while haunting her present. Fears filled her chest until she could barely breathe. Her first thought was to run and hide. Instead she forced herself closer, peeking through the crack in the partially open door.

Ma and Pa Hatfield really were here—and Jesse was with them. Please God, she begged, there must be some mistake. But she saw what she saw—and what she heard was even worse. While she had lain injured had Jesse betrayed her?

"Well, where is she?" Pa Hatfield demanded. "She ain't hurt or sick is she? The girl already missed most of the plantin' season. She has a lot to make up for."

Trinity cringed. The recollection of the never-ending chores made her back hurt and her muscles ache. Why would Jesse do this? Since the day they met he had always protected her.

Pa Hatfield scratched the back of his brutish neck,

then fiddled with his straw hat.

Jesse kept staring at the man as if he'd never seen a farmer before.

"She's nearby," Jesse said, "but Trinity's no longer your concern."

"What do you mean by that, mister?" Pa Hatfield straddled his legs and folded his beefy forearms across his barrel chest. "She belongs to us, and we gotta head back. The farm don't run itself you know. And the way you dragged us back here under armed guard, I ain't paying you no reward for finding her."

Is that why he'd done it—for the money? If so, he was out of luck. Coaxing eggs from a rooster would be simpler than getting money from Pa Hatfield.

How could this be happening? She had always stood by Jesse without question. He could at least afford her the same loyalty. And how could he still appear so noble as he delivered her back into the living nightmare from which she'd finally escaped.

"Like I said, mister, time's a wastin'. The hired hand ain't the only one interested in becoming her husband. We need to get that situation sorted out and proceed with the nuptials."

****

Throttling these two sorry excuses for humanity crossed Jesse's mind, but he couldn't make one misstep. This matter needed to be over and done with—legally and permanently. The Hatfields must never hurt Trinity again.

"Bring me Trinity," Pa Hatfield bellowed, snatching back the document Jesse held.

"Trinity's not going anywhere with you."

Mr. Hatfield bristled like a boar on the attack, but

he held his silence.

"Do somethin', Pa." The woman prodded her husband with an elbow to the ribs. "We didn't feed and tend that brat all these years only to lose her now when the biddin' on her will be the highest."

"Shut up, Ma."

Jesse balled his hands into fists. They talked about Trinity as if she were a prize heifer. How had she risen above such ignorance and cruelty? "You should take your husband's advice, Mrs. Hatfield. Selling people is against the law." Briggs could attest to that. "And the papers you're carrying were barely legal twenty years ago. They're certainly worthless now."

"What makes you so smart," Pa Hatfield sniped.

"A law degree from Harvard." That was the second time in the past few weeks those words had come out of his mouth. He was beginning to like the sound of them. Maybe opening a law practice in Prairie Ridge wasn't such a bad idea after all.

"Well I ain't had no fancy book learnin', but I know Trinity is under our care until she marries."

Ma Hatfield grunted in satisfaction.

The man's questionable document stated such but refuting the addendum would be easy enough. Still, better to play this out once and for all so these monsters finally understood they had no leg to stand on.

"Then you'll be glad to know she's to become my wife." Jesse touched his shirt pocket, comforted by the feel of the braided blonde hair coiled inside.

****

Trinity rushed into the room. Jesse caught her on the fly as she flung herself into his arms.

"Trinity…are you all right?"

"I am now."

"What in tarnation happened to her hair?" Mrs. Hatfield scorned.

"Never mind that." Mr. Hatfield waved his useless document threateningly, nearly hitting his wife in the face. "We never gave consent for her to marry you. Only a judge can overrule our authority, and I hear the circuit magistrate is locked in irons and on his way to Denver."

Jesse drew her arms down from around his neck. Then he tucked her around behind his back, as if to shield her.

"If you still insist on playing your useless game, Mr. Hatfield, then I'm happy to inform you the governor is still in town. I'm sure he would be happy to overrule you and officiate at the wedding."

Pa Hatfield took a step back, eyes dark with fury. If hate was a commodity, he'd be a rich man.

Jesse glared back at him. "Your document is only good for starting the next fire in your woodstove. Now I suggest you leave with great haste—before I do something I might regret. And in the future, if you value your pitiful selves, you will never again show your faces to me or Trinity or interfere in any way with our lives. Have I made myself clear?" Jesse rested one hand on the butt of the weapon he wore.

Pa Hatfield crumpled the paper and threw it at their feet. "She was useless when we got her, and she's good for nothing to the end." He slammed his hat on his head and stalked off leaving Ma Hatfield hurrying to catch up.

"I can barely believe what just happened. How did all this come about?" Transfixed Trinity stared at the retreating figures.

Jesse turned her around to face him. "Believe it. And believe me when I say I love you."

"I do believe you. And I love you too, Jesse."

"Good. Then the only question remaining is will you marry me?"

Overwhelmed by all the turn of events, she hesitated to respond.

"I'm sorry," he added. "I planned on proposing with flowers and candlelight—in some place much more romantic and intimate than the backroom of a saloon."

"I see. But now that I just learned there are multiple offers for my hand in marriage, perhaps I should consider my answer rather carefully?"

Jesse drew her close and kissed her with a hunger that sparked her own.

"Does that help in the decision making?"

She nodded trying to catch her breath. "Yes. Tell the governor I'm ready, willing, and able—and can hardly wait. But how is it Governor Adams is still in town?"

"Turns out his family lived here for a few years when he was growing up, so he decided to remain in Prairie Ridge to help get the town back on its feet. He organized a special platoon to try and locate the men and women Briggs sold into hard labor. And with the floodwaters receding, his soldiers are helping shore up the bridge."

"My goodness. All this happened in the short time I lay languishing in bed."

"Those days are over." He gave her a gentle, reassuring hug.

"But however did you convince the Hatfields to leave Middle Kiowa and come here?"

"The governor loaned me two soldiers to escort them, and one other person, back to Prairie Ridge. Heaven above, Trinity. I'm so sorry you had to live with such cruelty."

"I guess the point is, thanks to Etta, I did live. I miss her so very much."

"Come with me."

"But where are you taking me?"

"Never mind, just come along."

He took her hand and guided her back upstairs—this time into Mary June's room.

She glanced around, her gaze catching on the familiar figure standing near the window.

"It can't be—oh Etta, Etta."

The small, charming woman, wearing a fancy hat, turned in her direction, arms outstretched. Lord Byron lay on the floor nearby, tail thumping wildly.

Epilogue

Prairie Ridge, Colorado. Six months later

After Trinity left Middle Kiowa, the range wars had gotten worse, and Etta seriously contemplated selling the farm. Then when Jesse tracked her down, it seemed the perfect time to make the move.

Of course, living so close to town was quite a change. On occasion Etta still missed the wide-open spaces, but now she could visit her cousin in Denver when the desire struck—and more importantly, her wayward, rebellious angel would always be nearby.

Happy as could be, she rocked in her old chair on her new porch. "Well, Lord Byron. We certainly have the full-fledged family we always wanted. And a new beginning for all of us."

When the railroad spur never made it to Prairie Ridge, the town had declined into near poverty, making easy pickings for Briggs and his gang. Now, folks were moving here and setting up shop—like Jesse with his lawyering business. At least, that's what Etta read in the latest edition of the Prairie Ridge Review.

Along with Trinity, Jesse, and a few of the girls, Etta claimed part ownership of the abandoned railroad depot—which they had reworked into a respectable, profitable, and downright elegant boardinghouse named Great Expectations. You couldn't go wrong with

Dickens.

For peace and quiet, Etta had her own little apartment on the top floor, and her own space on the porch when she felt like company. And they called her the matriarch, which pleased her to no end. Lord Byron was the greeter and watch dog, and her big black cat kept the place mouse-free.

As it turned out, Annie liked to bake, Kate was quite the cook, and Petey worked in the vegetable garden and went hunting with Jesse. Camille embroidered the linens and took in alterations, and Lolly gave them all the best haircuts in town. Not to be left out, Mary June, her canaries singing in the parlor, used her organization skills to keep the staff on track and the place well stocked.

Being the best at numbers, Trinity tallied the boardinghouse books. And speaking of books, one thing they had all agreed upon was making a large main floor room into a library—one filled to overflowing and available to the public.

"Would you like another cup of tea, Etta?" Trinity glanced over from where she sat beside Jesse on the front porch step.

"No, thank you, dear heart. You just sit still. I'm fine. Everything is fine." Etta was delighted that the little girl in the apple tree had finally found the loving home she so deserved.

Trinity was aglow with being a wife, and so looking forward to motherhood. And who could blame her? Her husband was a devilishly handsome man, and smart to boot, and he treated her with great kindness.

Etta chuckled and watched Jesse toying with Trinity's blonde hair—a not infrequent pastime. After learning how Jesse and Trinity had met, she could understand why. What an adventure they'd had, and their lives had just begun.

Jesse kissed Trinity's cheek, then he settled one hand on her rounded belly.

Trinity smiled and covered his hand with hers.

If the babe was a girl, they promised to name her Etta, and she couldn't be more proud. If it was a boy, they'd chosen Jacob.

Etta glanced at the man coming up the walkway. Solomon—that was a good name too. He claimed to like poetry. Rocking gently back and forth, Etta gave Sol a shy smile.

Author's Note...

My story touches upon adoption fraud and human trafficking in 1888. But it wasn't new then, and sadly these practices continue today.

If you see, suspect, or are trapped in a trafficking situation, please call for help.

Colorado 24-hour confidential help line:
1-866-455-5075 or TEXT 720-999-9724
And Nationally 1-888- 373-7888
SMS: 233733 (Text "HELP" or "INFO")
Hours: 24 hours, 7 days a week
English, Spanish, and 200 more languages
Website: humantraffickinghotline.org

In case you were wondering...

The School of Mines opened in Golden, Colorado, in 1859. Early academic departments were drafting, physics, metallurgy, chemistry, and mining.

Pirates of Penzance was first performed in the Fifth Avenue Theatre in New York City on December 31, 1879.

Banks offering interest: Although not universal, the practice started around 1836.

New York Stock Exchange (NYSE) began in 1817.

Harvard law school: Founded in 1817, Harvard Law School is the oldest continually operating law school in the United States.

The Circus: Ringling Brothers World's Greatest Show was founded in Baraboo, Wisconsin, 1884. By 1888 they were traveling by train.

The terms "covert" and "criminology" were known and used by 1888. "Undercover," as used in the title, was not common until around 1920.

A word about the author…

Gini Rifkin's books follow characters who are courageous and passionate about life, and when they meet, sparks fly while danger often threatens. Her settings include the American West, Medieval and Victorian England, and contemporary fantasy.

When not writing, Gini has the privilege of caring for her menagerie of rescue animals including ducks, geese, goats, rabbits, donkeys, and cats. Her writing keeps her hungry to learn new things, and she considers family and friends her most treasured of gifts. So step back in time or into the future, where adventurous romance is waiting just for you.

Visit Gini at:

http://ginirifkin.blogspot.com